New Girl

the Further Adventures of Elinormal

to the fabulous, inspiring,
always kind Moore Girls ~
Cailin, Meghan, Brianna, and Kerry.

New Girl

the Further Adventures of Elinormal

Kate McCarroll Moore

A City of Light imprint

Cross Your Heart
A City of Light imprint

City of Light Publishing
266 Elmwood Ave. Suite 407
Buffalo, New York 14222

info@CityofLightPublishing.com
www.CityofLightPublishing.com

Book design by Ana Cristina Ochoa

ISBN 978-1-952536-34-2 (softcover)
ISBN 978-1-952536-35-9 (eBook)

Printed in Canada
10 9 8 7 6 5 4 3 2 1

Library of Congress Cataloging-in-Publication Data

Names: Moore, Kate McCarroll, author.
Title: New girl : the further adventures of Einormal / Kate McCarroll Moore.
Description: Buffalo, New York : Cross Your Heart, a City of Light imprint, [2022]
| Series: The Elinormal series ; book 2 | Audience: Ages 9-12. | Audience: Grades
4-8. | Summary: As seventh grade gets off to a rocky start, Elinor is balancing
friendships, old and new, while also unraveling the secrets behind her mother's
mysterious past.
Identifiers: LCCN 2021056627 (print) | LCCN 2021056628 (ebook) | ISBN
9781952536342 (trade paperback) | ISBN 9781952536359 (ebook) | ISBN
9781952536359 (epub) | ISBN 9781952536359 (mobi) | ISBN 9781952536359
(pdf)
Subjects: CYAC: Middle schools--Fiction. | Schools--Fiction. | Friendship--
Fiction. | Mothers and daughters--Fiction. | Secrets--Fiction. | LCGFT: Novels.
Classification: LCC PZ7.1.M6555 Ne 2022 (print) | LCC PZ7.1.M6555 (ebook)
| DDC [Fic]--dc23
LC record available at https://lccn.loc.gov/2021056627
LC ebook record available at https://lccn.loc.gov/2021056628

Contents

ONE

Nightmare

"Run, Elinor. Put some mustard on it!"

I was panting alongside my mother as we dashed through the airport from Concourse B to C, my backpack slamming against me with each step along the moving walkway.

Five minutes earlier we'd been dropped at the curb by her car service, only to find our gate had been changed to a whole other part of the airport. And the plane was leaving in twenty-four minutes.

"I'm running in heels for pity's sake. At least you can keep up with me. I'm not missing this flight because of you!"

"Excuse me. Excuse me, coming through," I shouted as I followed her and her rolling suitcase careening past the people standing still on the right.

It wasn't until we were wedged into our seats in coach, my backpack crammed beneath the seat in front of me, that I could finally breathe. And only then did I start to cry.

Today was supposed to be the first day of seventh grade.

"Now what? We made it. Why are you blubbering?"

I wiped my nose with the back of my hand and swallowed hard. "I'm just so sad about Grandma Ruth."

She patted my hand and said, "Oh, I know, kiddo. Me too, me too." Then she pulled her eye shade down, popped her earbuds in, and tipped her seat back as far as it could go.

I pulled out my sketchbook and started to draw. First, I sketched me in my first day of seventh grade outfit which I was now wearing on a plane to Oklahoma for my grandma's funeral. Then I tried to draw Grandma Ruth, but it was hard to remember what she looked like. I hadn't seen her since I was nine.

Just the night before, I had gone through my closet, trying on each new outfit in front of the mirror, trying to settle on the look I was going for – cool girl, sporty girl, brainy girl – finally landing on an orange minidress, denim jacket, and white sneakers that seemed to say, "just me, Elinor Malcolm, normal girl." I hung the dress in the bathroom, draped the jacket over the back of my desk chair, and put the sneakers next to my backpack which I emptied and rearranged fifty times. I checked my vision board and whispered each hope over and over.

- Get straight A's
- Go out for yearbook
- Become vegan
- Learn Spanish
- Make new friends

This was going to be my year. My best friend Christine and I had almost matching schedules and were going to be in three classes together. And her mom signed us both up to take a Saturday yoga class at The Healing HeARTs where my friend Indira works.

But then, just as I was getting ready to head for the bus, my mom let out a blood-curdling scream. I ran into her bedroom to find her on her knees, clutching her cell phone.

I helped her up and had her sit on the bed. Her face was pale and she was shaking.

"Mom, what is it? What happened?"

"It's Grandma Ruth," she whispered, "dead." She handed me the phone. "Call Dad and tell him we're on the next flight to Tulsa. And bring me an aspirin."

That set this nightmare in motion. Soon I was unpacking my backpack full of gel pens and labeled notebooks and a brand-new laptop, and replacing them with toiletries and underwear, and exchanging my first week of seventh grade for a funeral for a woman I barely knew.

By the time we landed and I took my phone off airplane mode, I had sixteen texts from Christine.

Where are you?

Are you sick?

We have science homework already.

Where are you?

The cafeteria smells disgusting.

We have to give speeches in English.

And read 8 books.

Where are you?

There's a new boy from Mexico or Modesto.

I forgot.

Sort of cute.

Tiff Tilton got braces.

Janna Faz got boobs.

Where are you?

Text me.

Are you ok?

My one and only first day of seventh grade was happening without me.

TWO

Darkness, Darkness

ulsa was the worst.

We landed in a thunderstorm. My dad's plane from Baltimore got diverted, so he didn't get there till the next day, and then he and my mom both headed to the funeral home to "make arrangements." I had to stay alone at my dead grandmother's house to accept deliveries of vases of flowers and completely inedible-looking brown casseroles.

That evening, after a long grey day alone having to answer the doorbell with a fake smile, my parents returned. As soon as they walked through the door, my mother went straight to bed and my dad headed to the kitchen to microwave one of the brown lumpy "covered dishes" dropped off by one of the many old ladies who lived on Grandma Ruth's street. "This is what's missing in California," he told me. "This is what it means to be neighborly. These people care about each other, not just themselves."

I thought that was weird. Our next-door neighbor, Mrs. Feinstein, drives me to school when I miss the bus, and she left a basket of lemons from her lemon tree on our front porch just last week. And the man across the street collects our packages when we're not home and makes us homemade pumpkin bread at Thanksgiving. Last year when he handed me a still-warm loaf wrapped in orange foil he told me, "I just love to pay it forward and show my gratitude to the good lord for this life. I bake a prayer and a little kindness into every loaf."

"He's probably just looking for an invite," my mom said when I set the bread on the table, but I think he's just a lonely old man being neighborly. And anyway, it would be nice to share our Thanksgiving with somebody else for a change instead of it being just the three of us. I bet Grandma Ruth shared Thanksgiving with all her neighbors.

I have to say, Grandma Ruth's house weirded me out a little. She had pictures of us everywhere. Stuck to the refrigerator with magnets, taped to her bedroom mirror, framed on the wall up the stairs and down the hall. We did not have one picture of her in our house. Not one.

The first night I passed out exhausted when I climbed into bed, but this second night I lay awake half the night in my mother's old room with its low ceiling and floral wallpaper that looked like eyes watching me in the dark. The floorboards creaked and it sounded like the walls were breathing. I kept trying to picture my mother at my age, lying in this bed, in this room. I wondered if back then she imagined leaving Oklahoma and becoming a big-shot lawyer and having me. I wondered why she hadn't visited her mom once in the last three years and why she never talked about her. I wondered if she'd ever tell me the truth.

The next day was the funeral. Just as we got to the cemetery, there was a huge clap of thunder and it began to pour. "Hear that?" my dad said, patting my hand in the back seat of the limo. "Your grandma's refusing to go quietly."

With that, my mom rested her head against the fogged-up window and began to cry, whole-body sobs that violently shook the backseat. "It's all right, Mims. Let it all out," my dad whispered, reaching behind me to rub my mom's shoulder.

There were lots of people dressed in black, standing under an awning by the gravesite. Standing and waiting. It was very hot inside the car.

My phone in my pocket vibrated and I sneaked a peek at the screen—a text from Christine.

Day 3 w/out an Elinor sighting. R U still alive?

I'm not sure why, but I started to cry again too. Maybe it was because of the rain. Rain always makes me cry. Sandwiched between my parents in the back of a long, black limousine, all of us mourning for different reasons, everything just felt so depressingly sad. My mom was now an orphan. My dad was missing an important meeting in Baltimore where he was supposed to be delivering the keynote address. And, I'd never get to have a first day of seventh grade. My whole life was happening back at school without me. Why did I have to be here? I didn't even really know my grandma, and now I never would.

A man carrying an enormous black umbrella appeared at the side of the limo and signaled for us to walk with him, so that's what we did. My mom got out first and walked alongside him under the umbrella while my dad walked behind me, holding his suit coat over my head. It didn't make a very good umbrella, but the rain was warm and I didn't mind. By the time the service was over, the sun was shining again and I didn't feel like crying anymore.

Back at the house filled with people I didn't know, I sat on the stairs and listened.

"Oh, my, that Elinor is the spitting image of her mother, isn't she?"

"Bet she has a wild streak just like her, too."

"Ruth was so proud of that girl."

"Remember that newspaper article she showed us all at Bridge last year?"

"Such a rebel!"

My phone vibrated again and I slipped it out to see the latest Christine text. Should I call the police? Three days and I still hadn't texted her back. What kind of a friend was I? I tucked my phone back into my pocket and made my way into the dining room. The table was covered with a white lace tablecloth, and decorated with tall vases of flowers and platters of little sandwiches and bowls of creamy salads. Someone must have come in and done all this while we were getting drenched at the cemetery.

While I was loading up a plate, a girl about my age sidled up alongside me. "That's my potato salad," she said, "made with your grandma's recipe. I'm Joelle by the way."

"Looks good," I said, pushing it around on my plate with a plastic fork. "How did you know her?"

"Grandma Ruth? Why, everybody knows her. She's everybody's grandma."

Joelle went on to tell me how Grandma Ruth invited all the neighbors in for Sunday dinner once a month and how she taught all the neighborhood kids how to play Scrabble and Pinochle and she taught a lucky few how to make the world's best potato salad with her secret recipe.

"She talked about you all the time. She'd say, 'My Elinor is just the same age as you. You'd be fast friends if she lived here. She's a dancer too.'"

"Actually, I'm more into yoga now," I said as my phone continued to buzz in my pocket. "And I'm going to be on yearbook."

"Cool," she said, spearing a pickle with a toothpick and pointing it at me. "Want to hang out sometime?"

"Thanks," I said, "but I'm leaving tomorrow." I started to walk away to find a place to finally text Christine back, to tell her I was sorry for making her worry and I'd be back on Saturday. I hoped she wouldn't have a new best friend by then.

"Well, what about now?" Joelle said as I headed for the back door. "What are you doing right now?"

THREE

Another Tree Girl

Joelle and I walked to the end of the block, and she told me about all the people who lived in each house. Mostly old people who'd lived here since my mom was a little girl. "They'd all usually be sitting out on their porches in the afternoon, but everybody's at your grandma's house now, telling stories and hugging your mom." I could not imagine my mom being hugged by anyone. But I couldn't imagine her crying either, and she'd been doing that ever since we got here.

Whenever someone on the street died, Joelle told me, a new young family would move in, paint the shutters and update the kitchen. She and her family had lived there since Joelle was six, and she said she'd kind of adopted my grandma as her own since her one grandma lived in England, and her other one died before she was born. She called my Grandma Ruth Grandma Ruth, too. "So, it's sort of like we're cousins, don't you think?" she asked.

I wasn't sure what I thought about that. It seemed like Joelle knew my grandma better than I did. And my grandma knew her better than she knew me, her own flesh and blood. I guess it would be sort of nice to have a cousin, but it was too late for that. My grandma was dead and we were flying home in the morning. I'd probably never see Joelle again.

We walked to the gas station on the next block, and Joelle bought us each a bottle of water. I was going to tell her that we tried not to ever drink bottled water because of plastics and the environment and junk, but the afternoon was sticky hot and I was really thirsty. "I'll show you my secret spot," she said as we rounded the corner. Up ahead was a tennis court and a playground that we walked past. An archway to our left announced "Crow Feather Park," and that's where we headed.

It was eerily similar to the park where I first met Indira last year. Joelle led me off the walkway to sit against an oak tree. "I'm a tree girl," Joelle said. "I like to sit here and think about how we need each other, you know, people and trees." I leaned back and closed my eyes, picturing the first time I saw Indira in the park back home, standing in tree pose. "You don't have to say anything if you don't want to," Joelle continued. "It's just nice to have someplace to breathe, you know?"

I did know. I remember walking away from the ballet studio last year and finding that park where I could think and write and draw and be myself. It's where I met Indira, where I discovered the bluebird of happiness, where I started to figure out who I was and what I was good at. I was going to tell Joelle all about that, but somehow, sitting there with her, I didn't need to say it.

"I'm glad I knew your Grandma Ruth," she said. "She loved trees too. She always said they were like spirits we could commune with. I can sort of feel her here now, can't you?"

I could not feel her there. I could not even picture what she looked like except for the black and white photo on the memorial card. And that was taken when she won a writing contest in 1992. She did not look like a grandma in that photo. She was young and beautiful with a big pouf of dark hair and crinkly eyes. I tugged a few blades of grass up and knotted them together into a bracelet, then slipped it on my wrist. "What was she like?"

Joelle looked at me. I took the bracelet off and passed it to her and she slipped it on. Then I started on a new one.

"I mean you probably knew her in a different way than I did," I said.

"I guess. Are you going to see who keeps texting you?"

I was trying to ignore the constant ding in my pocket, but I guess it was hopeless.

"Probably Christine. My best friend. She thinks I've died or something 'cause I'm missing our first week of school."

Joelle tried to convince me to text her back, but I really didn't want to. I didn't want to spoil the afternoon with Joelle by focusing on life back at Valley Middle School. And I wasn't sure why. Maybe it's a family trait. One time my mom told me that she had this amazing ability to compartmentalize. "When I'm at work," she told me, "I don't think about anything else. Everything else disappears."

"You think about me though, right?" I said.

"Oh, for goodness sake Elinor," she'd replied as she continued folding towels, before handing me a warm stack to put away, "the world does not revolve around you."

I reluctantly pulled my cell phone out of my pocket, but it was not another text from Christine. It was, instead, a string of texts. Like I said, not from Christine.

Hey.

Nerd alert.

Guess what.

Get this.

What kind of Wren is not a bird?

The string-of-texts sender was Indira, aka Tiffany Woo, daughter of Carpool Mom, aka Shoshana Finkle-Woo. Her texts were always a little hard to decipher.

I showed it to Joelle. "Weird! What's that mean?"

The truth is, I had no idea. But I knew it must be important.

I held my phone above us and snapped a selfie of me and Joelle sitting side-by-side underneath the tree. I sent a text back to Indira. Hey, girl. Oklahoma days. Just me. And my cousin Joelle. And Grandma Ruth's spirit. #TulsaTreegirls #Oakiespirit #Birdnerds

Another ding. Oklahoma? What the fudge?!

I texted back about my grandma's funeral and missing the first day, now the first week of seventh grade.

It took Indira a lot of wordcrazy texts back and forth before she explained that the reason for her nerd alert text was that a woman her mom profiled in the Santa Marita Spirit last month wants to meet us. Her name is Liza Wren and she writes novels in verse. Indira wrote that she's a real up-and-comer in the literary world. And now she wants to write a book about the three of us.

My head was spinning. *A book? About us?*

Yuppers! I'm ready for my close up, Mr. Demille, she replied.

I passed the phone to Joelle, and she burst out laughing. "Text her back that you'll meet her on Sunset Boulevard."

I felt like I was caught in the middle of some enormous joke and I didn't know the punchline. When I texted Joelle's message back, Indira replied with a winking emoji. Then she said she had to run, but she'd let Christine know I was safe and had just been too distraught by my grandma's death to text her back.

I felt a little pang of guilt when she wrote that. Indira always knew how to make things right. But why hadn't I texted Christine back this whole time? I hoped she'd forgive me. I guess she'd have to now if we were going to be starring in a book together.

The sun sank lower in the sky and a little breeze came up as I shared the details about last year with Joelle. How I quit ballet and met Indira and then how everything kept connecting in weird ways. I told her about my cat that had to go live with Christine, and about Christine's mom taking us to The Healing HeARTs, and about Indira performing my poem, and Indira's mom being the newspaper columnist that I'd been writing to, and how her name was really Tiffany not Indira, and about me and Christine and Indira working on a new poetry dance.

"No wonder Grandma Ruth thought we'd be friends," Joelle said when I finished. "And no wonder a big-time author wants to write about you guys. I'd read that story!"

"It's not a story though," I said, my head still spinning. "It's my life."

FOUR

Guilty

It's hard to believe how your life can keep making these 180 degree turns, out of your control, and you just keep bouncing along, not sure what's going to happen next. Just a week ago my whole life had been upended by a phone call. How I had hated missing the beginning of seventh grade in California, and now I was just as sad about leaving Oklahoma! Just a week ago, I didn't know Joelle existed, and now it felt like we were cousins, like we'd been friends forever. Life is just a never-ending string of coincidences and surprises.

When I got home from the park, the house was empty except for two ladies in the kitchen putting things in Tupperware.

"I'm glad she decided to stay. It's only right."

"Indeed," the other one replied. "So glad you talked some sense into her."

"Not sense. Guilt. Good old-fashioned guilt. Works every time."

They both nodded and clucked like hens, as they continued scooping leftovers into plastic tubs.

I stood frozen on the other side of the kitchen door.

"Poor Ruth. Shut out of her daughter's life like that."

"At least now she'll have some peace."

"Indeed."

"There's plenty here for her to eat all week. Nice work, Effie."

"Well, I guess our work here is done then."

"Let's call it a day. Will you get the lights?"

"Indeed."

And that's how I found out that my mom was planning to stay in Oklahoma to get the house "closed-up" while my dad and I flew back to California without her.

That night, I couldn't sleep, thinking about all that had happened in the space of a week. My grandmother's funeral, my friendship with Joelle, and the promise of our story becoming a book. All these different worlds stretching and colliding and connecting. Sometimes when I can't sleep, I like to sit in my closet and write. I don't know why, but it's something I've done since I was really little. I tiptoed across the room in the dark, the wallpaper eyes staring at me, opened the closet, and flicked on the overhead light. I took my notebook and pencils out of my packed duffel, and leaned against the back wall, where it felt safe and peaceful.

I wrote a poem about oak trees and another one about funeral rain. It felt so good to be getting my feelings down like that. I was already starting to think about ways Indira and Christine could help me combine and choreograph them, when I spotted a box tucked in the very back of the closet. "Don't touch!" it said in big bubble letters. "Fragile." I ran my hand across the top where a piece of the packing tape had come unstuck. I tugged it a little, then a little bit more, until the box was no longer closed.

It was like a treasure chest – filled with things from when my mom was a teenager - her high school yearbook, a plastic bag filled with photographs, and a bunch of t-shirts decorated with pictures of '90s rock stars like Madonna and Gwen Stefani. At first I couldn't believe those things belonged to Marsha Malcolm who used to be Marsha Frisbie. But there it was—undeniable proof. A yearbook with her name written in large loopy letters inside the front cover, photographs that looked eerily just like me, but sporting a pile of blond hair and puffy bangs, posing with a bunch of people I'd never seen before. And one very handsome dark-haired boy in picture after picture, always standing pressed up close, his arm draped casually around her shoulders, her waist, or clutching her arm as if to say, "mine."

I told myself it wasn't stealing when I decided to take them. I needed to know why my mom and Grandma Ruth were estranged. Maybe it could help me understand her better. That's what I told myself. But if I'm being honest, I was also curious to find out about her and that cute boy. And those amazing t-shirts that she was wearing in the photos were right here in this box, folded in little pink and purple and yellow fabric squares! There was nothing fragile packed away here, unless, I thought, as I lifted them out of the box one by one, and spread them across the floor, she'd meant her memories.

I unzipped my packed duffel, shoved in the yearbook, the photos, and the folded the t-shirts, along with my notebook, and set it by the door for the morning. Then I tiptoed back to bed, across the creaky floorboards, and fell right to sleep.

I waited downstairs with my duffel packed with secrets while my dad called for an Uber. My mom was already up and dressed in a sweatsuit, piling leather-bound books onto the dining room table. She had set up an appointment for later that afternoon with an antiques dealer to come look through the china and assess the ancient wooden furniture that filled every room. "There's not a thing I want in this house," she told me when she broke the news that she was staying in Oklahoma to sell the house, something I already knew from the neighbors. "Not a thing."

I gave her a quick hug as my dad called out, "Car's here."

"Wish me luck!" she said as we headed out the door.

I waved at Joelle's house even though I knew she'd still be fast asleep in her room on the second floor, and I wondered if I'd ever see her again, now that we were selling Grandma Ruth's house. I took a wistful look at the long stretch of small houses with their bright front doors, all lined up close together like a group of friends, and whispered goodbye to Tulsa as the driver whisked my duffel bag of secrets out of my hand and tossed it into the trunk with a thud.

On the flight home, I snuggled into my dad's shoulder as he worked on his laptop and did the crossword puzzle in the in-flight magazine. My duffel bag was now stored right above me in the overhead bin and I wanted desperately to write in my journal but I couldn't chance opening it to reveal my mom's secrets which now belonged to me packed inside. What would he say if he saw those photographs, or if a pink Madonna tumbled out? Would he recognize his once-young wife standing on tiptoes next to such a handsome boy? Had he ever seen her wearing Gwen Stefani instead of her velour sweatsuit or her navy business suit? I wanted to ask him, but I knew I couldn't, so I closed my eyes and pretended to sleep.

FIVE

Hey, New Girl!

Christine was waiting for me in the front quad, surrounded by people I didn't know. She gave me a big hug and whispered, "Sorry," as I shyly entered the circle. All the girls, including Christine, were wearing yoga pants and boots, and there I stood in my minidress and sneakers, my first day of seventh grade outfit. I felt my face turning pink as all eyes turned to me.

"Hey, who's the new girl?" I shifted to see a boy standing on the edge of our circle. One lone boy in a sea of girls. One curly black-haired boy with an amazing dimple and two brown eyes flecked with gold. Staring right at me.

"She's not new you, doofus," Christine said. "This is Elinor. Remember, I told you about her?"

"Yeah? Well, she's new to me," he replied, then took a step closer to me and ran his hand through his dark curls. "Hey, new girl."

I couldn't speak. Like literally, opened my mouth and nothing came out. Some of the girls started to giggle, and I stood there turning pinker in my short orange dress which now felt way too short.

Luckily, that's when the bell rang and everyone headed inside. "See you around, new girl," he shouted over the din as we made our way inside.

"I should have warned you," Christine said as we walked to class. "That's Manuel. Remember I told you about him? The new boy from Modesto?"

"I thought you said Mexico." I tugged on my dress, trying to make it longer.

"Yeah, well I wasn't sure. But it's Modesto. He's the one that's new here. And he thinks he's God's gift."

We walked into homeroom, and Christine drifted right to her seat. I stood there awkwardly as the room filled up. School had already been in session for a week. All the seats had been assigned and the groups had been picked. I *was* the new girl.

The teacher looked up when the second bell rang and I was still standing there. It was Ms. Loveless, who had the misfortune of being given a name that surely matched her destiny. Ms. Loveless taught advanced math and computer science. She had a bit of a mustache and she never smiled although she had an incredibly loud and inappropriate laugh. She was famous at Valley Middle School. I was glad I would only have to see her for ten minutes every morning during homeroom.

"You must be new. I'll have to get you a chair from next door. Tell me your name."

She looked back down at her computer screen.

"Elinor," I croaked. "Elinor Malcolm." More giggles.

"Elinormal what? Oh, here you are. Malcolm, right? Well, you can just sit on the counter today," she said pointing to the counter I was leaning against in embarrassment. "I'll have a chair for you tomorrow."

If I was wearing yoga pants, I could hop right on up there. But again, my dress was too short for hoisting myself onto a classroom counter. "I'll just stand," I said. "I like standing." And then I stood there, all pastel pink face and orange dress and what I now realized were very pasty white legs, looking like a creamsicle melting into a pool of insignificance. The clock ticked above me, as the giggles subsided and everyone forgot I was there. Welcome to seventh grade, I thought to myself. Welcome to another year of me.

When the final bell rang, I told Christine I was still suffering from jet lag and I'd catch up with her tomorrow, then made a mad dash for the bus. I leaned my head against the cold glass and closed my eyes, nearly drifting off on the way home, as the jumble of images from the day swirled in my head. Christine and the rest of the seventh-grade girls in their shiny yoga uniforms, Ms. Loveless in her permanent scowl, and the cutest boy I've ever seen following close behind as I scurried down the hall.

Me, painfully aware of my new girl-didn't-get-the-memo look, in a short orange dress amid a sea of cliquey confident yoga girl coolness. Me, Elinormal, not cool once again.

SIX

Whatever Happened to Marsha Frisbie?

The pile of treasures from my mom's closet was waiting for me at home after school. I'd shoved everything under my bed when we got back from Oklahoma, planning to go through it all piece by piece, and now I could. My dad had told me this morning that he'd be at the office late catching up on everything he'd missed while we were away. I had the whole afternoon and evening to myself, so I searched for '90s music on my phone, and got to work.

One thing you should know about me is that I have a whole stash of empty notebooks on my bookshelf. I'm kind of a notebook fiend. I spent a while sorting through them all to find the perfect one for this project, and chose one with a plain white cover that I could decorate later. For now, I just labeled it *Before She Was Mom.*

I pulled out the t-shirts and lined them up across the floor. Madonna. Gwen. Alanis. Posh. Sheryl. Jewel. Then I searched through the photos matching up the t-shirts on the floor to the photos they appeared in.

I opened my journal to the first page and wrote, "What do I know about her?"

I studied the floor, then went back to the journal. "She liked music."

I piled those pictures on top of the shirts they matched up with. She must have liked Madonna best because there were seven pictures of my mom wearing that same shirt in my Madonna stack.

"Especially Madonna."

I pulled the yearbook for Central High, 1996 out from underneath the bed and ran my hand across the embossed leather cover. Opened it to her signature, Marsha Frisbie, then started flipping through, looking for her picture. There she was, smiling in an off-the-shoulder drapey black gown and pearls, wedged between Jeremy Franks and Lydie Frisk.

"She had style."

I turned the pages slowly, reading all the personal notes written to Marshie and Marshmallow and Frizzy. Notes like, *don't ever change* and *stay as sweet as you are* and *don't do anything I wouldn't do.*

"She had lots of nicknames."

I flipped through a few more pages.

"And lots of friends."

I kept slowly turning the pages and reading along in amazement.

Curt is such a lucky duck.

Good luck with Curt next year.

Let's make it a summer to remember, love Curtis.

That last message scribbled next to his picture in a tuxedo, his dark wavy hair covering one eye.

"Whatever happened to Curt(is)?" I jotted.

Below that I wrote, "Whatever happened to Marsha Frisbie?"

That night I had the weirdest dream. I was living in my Grandma Ruth's house in Oklahoma with my glamorous, long-haired mom. She walked around the house smiling and singing all day. I had a pet duck named Marshmallow who lived in my closet. At first my dad was my dad, but then he turned into the handsome dark-haired boy with his arm around my mom in all the pictures. In my dream he was driving me to school with Joelle and Christine and Indira in the back seat. He kept saying, "Remember to be good, girls. Stay sweet. Don't ever change."

When we pulled up to school, our car had turned into a school bus and the bus driver had turned into Manuel, the new boy from Modesto. We all started running toward a pack of 8th grade girls in '90s music t-shirts blocking the entrance as the school bell rang.

I sat up like a shot. My phone alarm was ringing under my pillow. I was no longer dreaming. Time for school for real.

You know how when you have a weird dream it lingers? There's a sort of cloudy feeling that you can't shake? That's what happened when I got to school for my second day of seventh grade. I'd been home from Oklahoma for three days, and I felt more exhausted than ever. I didn't believe in jet-lag, but I definitely had some-kind-of-lag by the time I entered the quad wearing my pink paisley yoga pants and my mom's old Madonna t-shirt. I saw Christine and for a minute wondered where Joelle was. Oh yeah, Oklahoma. Then, from the behind me, that already familiar voice shouted, "Hey, new girl!" I spun around, half expecting to see him behind the wheel of the school bus parked there. Weird.

When we walked into homeroom. Ms. Loveless said, "Oh look. It's the material girl!" No one laughed, but she let out a startling snort. Then she said, "Oh drat—can you go next door and ask Mr. Berg if he has an extra chair?"

I just stood there, not realizing at first that she was talking to me as the room filled up and she went back to taking attendance.

"Or you can just lean on the counter again if you'd rather. Up to you."

I wondered how some people could be so clueless. I wondered if she was different in high school. Did she have long wavy hair and wear pearls for her senior picture? Did she have a favorite singer? Did a dark-haired boy ever casually drape his arm across her shoulder? I couldn't imagine it.

I leaned against the counter and reached into the pocket of my jacket to rub the little lucky bluebird from Indira that I always carry. I tried to picture happiness as the clock ticked off the minutes till I'd be released from homeroom and could push my way through the crowded corridor with Christine, hoping that today would be better than yesterday. Hoping to sit near Manuel, the new boy from Modesto who appeared in my dreams and called me New Girl.

SEVEN

It's Madonna

he loudspeaker at the front of the room crackled to life, making that familiar staticky sound, and a high-pitched voice filled the classroom. It was seventh period art, one of the only classes I didn't share with Christine. She was in band.

"Hey there, Valley Cats, it's Tuesday, and here are today's announcements."

I doodled in my sketchbook, as the irritating voice droned on.

I stopped mid-doodle at the final announcement.

"Yearbook meets today at 3:00 in the library. Mr. F says all are welcome."

Mr. F was the coolest teacher in the whole school. I felt like I'd been given a shot of adrenaline. I pulled out my phone and sent a quick under-the-desk text to my dad. Taking the late bus. Yearbook tryouts today.

Christine was waiting for me outside the library along with two girls. All of them were whispering and swinging their flute cases as I approached. "Oh, hi," said the tallest one, "you're the new girl! I'm Sasha."

"She's not new," Christine said. "Remember? She was in your homeroom last year. This is Elinor."

"Okay," Sasha said, transferring her flute case to her other hand like it was heavy and her hand needed a rest. "You don't play an instrument?"

Before I could answer, another band girl walked up. She pointed at me and said, "Who's that?"

"It's Elinor from last year, Brit," Sasha told her.

"Duh," replied Brit, the band girl. "I mean who's that you're wearing? Katy Perry?"

"No way!" It was the other flute girl who'd been standing there when I walked up. "That's Dua Lipa. Right?"

Christine rolled her eyes.

"Actually," I said, "it's Madonna."

"Oh, I've heard of her," Sasha said.

With that, the library door swung open and instead of the wonderful Mr. F standing there, we were greeted by the less than wonderful Ms. Loveless.

It turns out that you don't actually have to try out for yearbook. You just have to show up and you're in. I looked around at the dozen other kids crowded around the long library table. A few eighth graders who worked on it last year, me and Christine and the three other band girls (Sasha, Brit, and Lucy), a couple of other girls who I didn't know but who seemed to know everyone, and one lone sixth grader, McHenry Plouffe–the only boy.

Ms. Loveless sat on the edge of a table facing us, taking a noisy sip through a plastic straw.

"Where's Mr. F?" one of the eighth graders asked. "He's our advisor."

"Was your advisor, Missy, emphasis on the was." There was that snorty laugh again. "The basketball team needed a coach, and need I say more?"

"But he knows all about yearbook. He's an English teacher." Missy's voice cracked, and Ms. Loveless cut her off with look.

"Well, I guess we're lucky to have this crackerjack return squad of eighth graders to show us the ropes then, aren't we?" She took another noisy slurp. "Let's get started."

The table erupted in not so quiet whispers. One of the eighth-grade girls rose as spokesperson, and cleared her throat. "The announcement said *Mr. F. says all are welcome.* That's false advertising."

A chorus of *yeahs* and *no fairs* rang out.

Now it was Ms. Loveless who looked like she was about to cry. She scooted back further on the table, her stockinged feet (where on earth were her shoes?)

dangling in mid-air. "Well, then," she clapped her hands together and then held them clasped awkwardly in front of her before continuing, "who's ready to get to work on Valley Middle School's best yearbook ever?" Snort.

The afternoon ended up being okay because 1) Nobody quit, even after the eighth graders threatened to because 2) Ms. Loveless had pizza delivered and because 3) we got to look through a bunch of old yearbooks and comment on the hair and clothes that looked weird and outdated, especially on the "best dressed" page.

McHenry Plouffe, who was wearing a polo shirt with a little puppy stitched near the collar and neon gym shorts said, with a mouthful of pizza, "Do you think someday kids might sit around and make fun of our clothes?" and Ms. Loveless said, in a super sincere tone, "No way. Your style will undoubtedly set the bar for generations to come." He stood up at that and took a bow, making us all laugh right along with the ear-piercing cackle of our replacement advisor.

EIGHT

Let the Weekend Begin!

id you ever notice that no matter how your week is going, Friday always feels different?

Friday! Exciting! Exhilarating! Extraordinary! Some Fridays are all that, and then some.

Last Friday, I was discovering the lost treasure of Marsha Frisbie in an off-limits box in the back of my mother's childhood closet. Last Friday, I was writing Joelle's name in my book of true friends after Indira and Christine. Last Friday, I was just days away from meeting the boy who called me New Girl, and made my heart pound.

And now it was Friday again. Maybe the best Friday of my entire life. I'm not sure what order to put these events in – it feels like they should all be number one.

1. Christine invited me to spend the night at her house so we could work on our poems.

1. We're going to meet up with Indira at The Healing HeARTs tomorrow to work on our choreography (I know that's technically Saturday, but the anticipation is all wrapped up in Friday!)

1. Indira's mom is introducing us to the famous writer Liza Wren at lunch tomorrow (again, anticipation is everything. Felt like I could jump right out of my skin when I opened the text this morning.)

1. Manuel, the new boy from Modesto, got a schedule change. He's moving to my 3rd period Spanish class on Monday.

1. There is an empty seat next to me, and guess who's going to fill it?

I love Fridays!

NINE

Pink

Spending the night at Christine's is like going to Six Flags. There is noise and commotion and laughter everywhere, all the time. And snacks! When we came in from school, her mom was in the kitchen making homemade pizza. I mean, like real pizza with dough from scratch. Christine scooped up the cat that was sitting on the counter and handed him to me. "Bari misses you!" she said as the cat squirmed free and high-tailed it out of the room. I could hardly believe this was Bari, my cat that Christine adopted last spring when I found out how allergic my mom is to cat fur. How do snuggly little kittens turn into fat skittish cats so quickly?

Mrs. Corrales gave us each a big hug and told us to help ourselves to a snack. "Slim pickins since Michael and

Matteo beat you to it, but you're welcome to whatever's there," she said laughing. "Those boys will eat us out of house and home!" The door to the back yard was wide open and Christine's brothers could be seen and heard tossing a frisbee back and forth under the trellis while the two dogs barked and ran back and forth across the lawn, launching themselves into the air with each toss.

"Chrissy, can you shut that door and grab your laundry off the table when you go upstairs? And Elinor, be a love and grab those towels and deposit them in the upstairs bathroom, would you?"

Christine grabbed an open bag of chips from the pantry and her laundry from the kitchen table, while I grabbed the folded towels, and we headed to her room at the top of the stairs. She was so excited to show me that her dad had recently painted one wall bright pink. "You're going to love this, Elinor. Sit down and close your eyes." I plopped down in the beanbag next to her bed.

"Keep them closed," she said. Her bird squawked in its cage in the corner. "Oh, be quiet, Elbird."

"What's the first line of your funeral rain poem again?"

"My grandmother left this world drenched in sky tears," I whispered, the words catching in my throat.

"Chills," said Christine. "Amazing line, Miss Poet. Hold still for another minute. You'll see why."

There was the sound of scratching that I thought was Elbird in his cage, but it turns out it wasn't.

When I opened my eyes, Christine was bouncing on the balls of her feet in place, pointing to the pink wall. "Ta-da!"

My poetry line was written across the wall in beautiful script, under a rain cloud.

"Your mom will kill you!" I blurted.

She started to laugh. "It's chalkboard paint. You're supposed to write on it."

My mouth was wide open as I stood up and ran my hand across my words painted there. I said a few unintelligible things like *wha?* and *buh* before I squeaked out, "I love it."

"Well, good," she said, "'cause I thought maybe we could work on putting some lines of poetry on the wall tonight and then Tik-Tok-ing ourselves or something."

My awesome Friday night got a whole lot more awesome. And we hadn't even had the pizza yet.

After dinner, we took leftover pizza and popcorn to Christine's room and decorated her wall with my words and her drawings. Then we filmed each other reciting and posing in front of our mural—Christine had a program on her computer that let us add music and splice our little videos into a cool minifilm that we sent to Indira. She texted back and said she'd have a yoga-ish dance choreographed to go along with it by the time we met up at The HealingHeARTs in the morning. We could film ourselves doing the dance and then layer that into the video.

The stars are born! Indira texted before we called it a night and finally turned out the light. And I've been thinking—we need a name. Sleep on this one, chickadees. What about PoetryInMotionArts? We could call ourselves PIMA for short.

I wrote it on the wall above my poetry, and took a picture with my phone. When I wrote the word Poetry, it looked like this: PoetRy. That's when I had my genius moment—at least that's what Indira called it when Christine texted her back with my discovery. What if we call ourselves PRIMA instead? I said when it popped out at me. PoetRyInMotionArts.

Yeah, like prima ballerinas except we're prima something else.

PRIMA Yogarinas! The deal is sealed! Indira texted. And that was that. We were officially the three PRIMA Yogarinas.

I settled myself on the air mattress on Christine's floor, the moonlight shining on the mural we had made on her pink wall. I tried closing my eyes but it seemed impossible to fall asleep between the bird noises and the cat scratching at the bedroom door to come in and out, her brothers running up and down the stairs, and the excitement of having a name for our project. Maybe Liza Wren would even call our book *The Prima Yogarinas*. Our book! We were going to be famous!

TEN

Reunion

Christine and I were both up before the sun, even though we had spent half the night wide awake. We raced down the stairs to find her mom already up making cinnamon rolls, her dad in the yard putting up a new basketball hoop with the boys, the dogs running in circles, and the cat—my old cat—sleeping in the middle of the table. Could you imagine Bari being allowed to have cinnamon dreams on the kitchen table in my house? I know he's happier here, even though I miss him. I'm happier here too, if you want to know the truth.

While we were eating breakfast, my phone dinged in my pocket. Then it dinged again.

"You can get it," Mrs. Corrales said as I felt my face turning red. "It might be important."

I knew it was rude to look at your phone at the table, but I thought maybe it was Indira. Or maybe even Joelle from Oklahoma, so I slid my phone out and took a quick look.

"Oh, it's my dad," I said. "I have to call him. May I be excused?"

"Did you say you want to be diffused?" Matteo asked as he and Michael dissolved in laughter. "Diffused, get it?"

"Don't be rude, boys," Mr. Corrales said.

"Is everything all right?" Mrs. Corrales and Christine asked at the same time as I raced to the living room. Both dogs were asleep on opposite ends of the sofa. I had to move a pile of books off a chair to sit down. My dad answered on the first ring which meant he was waiting for me to call back – it must be important.

He told me that my mom was on her way home from Tulsa as a surprise so he'd be coming to get me and then we could head to the airport to pick her up. He was making dinner reservations at our favorite restaurant tonight so we could have a little family reunion, just the three of us. I wanted to explain that I had a big day planned in the city with Christine and her mom, but I couldn't. And I didn't mention the PRIMA Yogarinas or the meeting with the author, because I knew he wouldn't understand. Couldn't understand. I just repeated that this was a really important day for me.

"Don't you think seeing your mom is important, Ellie-bear? She's missed you so much."

I pictured those two Tulsa ladies packing food in Tupperware in Grandma Ruth's kitchen the week before. *Guilt. Good old-fashioned guilt. Works every time.*

I walked back to the kitchen slowly, listening to the sound of laughter ringing through the house. I stood in the doorway for a few minutes taking it all in.

"Elinor, what's wrong, sweetie. You look like you've seen a ghost."

"I have to go," I squeaked. "My dad's on his way to get me."

Let me just say, you could probably guess how the rest of my day was going to go. My mom's plane was delayed so we had to circle the airport a million times until I felt like I was going to be sick. I said, "Why don't we just go home and mom can take the car service when she lands?"

He didn't answer for a minute, then said in his quiet voice, "Elinor, your mother just lost her mother. Can you imagine how that feels? And then she had to spend another week by herself going through all those memories in the house she grew up in. Have a little compassion."

In my head I was thinking *the airport is so close to the The HealingHeARTs—you could drop me off there now, come back to pick up Mom, and Christine's mom would have me home in time to go to dinner as a family—just the three of us.* But there it was again, that guilt. So instead, I just took in a big gulp of air (Indira called it a cleansing breath), and said, "You're right. I wasn't thinking. Ok."

When we finally saw her standing on the curb, she was dwarfed by a stack of shiny black suitcases. Even though she'd said there was nothing in that house that she wanted, she went ahead and bought and filled two new suitcases with stuff that she said was too good to part with. It couldn't all fit in the trunk so I had to sit in the back squished beside her regular suitcase, with my legs draped over a stuffed leather duffel on the floor of the car. "It'll be worth the discomfort, Elinor. Wait till you see what I found in the attic." So that's what that musty smell was.

Then she turned around from the front seat and winked at me. "Oh, and remind me when we get home, there's something from your little friend in there too."

"Joelle?"

"Well, of course, Joelle. How many friends did you make during your grandmother's funeral?" The way she said it was so, I don't know, disappointed, I guess. Like what kind of a person goes off to a park and has fun while their grandmother is being buried? At least that's how it sounded.

By the time we got home more than an hour later she was too exhausted from her week of getting Grandma Ruth's house ready to sell and her flight being delayed and lugging all those heavy suitcases to the curb because we were circling the airport instead of meeting her at the baggage claim like she'd expected, and then all the Saturday traffic because of whatever, so instead of unpacking, she went straight to bed.

"You know what we can do, Ellie-bear? How about if I order us something from EatUp? You want Chinese? Or Sushi? Thai? What do you feel like?" my dad asked as he dragged the last of the suitcases into the front hallway.

"I thought we were going to La Tratoria? Remember? For our little family reunion? That's what I feel like, if you really want to know." I plunked down on the bottom step and stared at the pile of heavy suitcases waiting to be carried upstairs.

My dad patted the top of the banister and sat down next to me on the stairs.

"Listen, Elinor. This is not how we thought the day would go. But we've got to make the best of it. We can try again tomorrow."

Sometimes I feel like such a wimp. I wanted my present from Joelle. I wanted my special dinner. I wanted to be at The Healing HeARTs choreographing my poems with Christine and Indira and meeting the author Liza Wren who was going to write a book about the PRIMA Yogarinas. I wanted my mom to be smiling and swinging her hair like she was doing in those pictures I found in her closet. Where did that person go?

I leaned my head into my dad and whispered, "I was having cinnamon rolls at Christine's this morning. Her mom made them from scratch."

He kissed my forehead. "Sounds delicious."

"And everybody was talking and laughing. Her brothers were having a contest to see who could make the goofiest face."

He put his arm around my shoulder and pulled me closer. "Sounds like a great way to kick off the weekend."

"And then you called…" I swallowed hard.

"And?"

"I was supposed to go to the city with Christine and her mom. We had it all planned." I don't know why I was still whispering, but I was.

I thought maybe he'd get mad or something because I was being selfish and not showing compassion. But he didn't. He put his hand under my chin so I had to look up at him. His eyes looked watery. "Oh, my girl. I'm so sorry. I completely forgot. Just totally forgot." At that, he stood up, pushed up his sleeve, and looked at his watch with his thinking face. "How about we let your mother rest and we keep that reservation, you and me? You can tell me all about the day you almost had, and we can figure out how to not let that happen again. What do you say?"

I nodded, then stood up too, and realized I was smiling.

"And tonight when we get home, how about if we have a little movie marathon? Have you ever seen *West Side Story?*" He started snapping his fingers and doing this weird little dance over to the closet to grab his jacket. That's the thing about my dad. He always knows how to make things better.

"I'll be right back," I said, racing up the stairs to wash my face and brush my teeth. "Wait for me."

ELEVEN

Love Story

We stayed up till almost midnight watching movies in the dark. After West Side Story ended, he told me about Romeo and Juliet and how that was the original love story. Then he clicked around until he found it on some oldies station, and we watched it in silence and both had a good cry at the end. Juliet was so gorgeous in that white night gown, and Romeo sort of reminded me of Manuel with his beautiful dark eyes and his boldness.

"Can people really fall in love that fast?" I asked, wiping my eyes with a napkin as my dad switched off the TV.

"I asked my mom the same thing when I watched it with her when I was just about your age," he said. "She and my dad were going through a nasty divorce, and she assured me that people could not. But I'm not so sure about that." He set the remote back on the coffee table and picked up our empty glasses and the half-eaten cheesecake wilting in the take-out box from La Tratorria.

"Really?" I gathered up the dessert plates and used napkins and followed him into the kitchen.

"Absolutely! After all, I fell head over heels in love the moment I laid eyes on you, didn't I? You, with your cone shaped head and your little arms and legs coated in white gunk, screaming like a banshee. You were the most beautiful thing I'd ever seen! So, love at first sight, I'm gonna go with yes."

The kitchen was dark except for one little lamp glowing on the sideboard, bathing my dad in golden light as he stood at the sink. "I'll take care of these dishes," he said, "and you, my dear, had better hightail it up to bed before your mother finds out I let you stay up half the night watching sappy movies and gorging on sugar."

At first I thought it was bees. The buzz buzz buzz of my phone woke me out of a deep sleep. It was still pitch black outside. Five-thirty am.

Hey girl.
You like?

Oops. Sorry.

Forgot the time difference.

It took a minute to register.

Time difference. Hey girl. Could only be Joelle.

I'm up, I texted back.

Early bird! So, you like?

What?

The thing I made you.

The thing? I yawned, squinting at the screen.

Yeah, the, um, she didn't give it to you, did she?

That's when I remembered. "There's something from your little friend," my mom had said in the car on the way home from the airport. But that was before my day was ruined and she went to bed and my dad hauled the unpacked suitcases into the guest room and we stayed up late and my day was salvaged and I fell asleep and forgot. My head was spinning.

Uh, no. Not yet.

Oh.

What else was there to say?

It's still dark here, I typed. Later. And with that, I shoved my phone back under my pillow and jumped out of bed.

TWELVE

Snark

The hallway was completely dark so I felt my way on tiptoes and gently pushed open the door to the guest room. The suitcases were lined up neatly in the middle of the room, the full moon casting weird shadows that made them look dangerous, like stealthy wild animals ready to pounce. I crept toward them, looking over my shoulder and trying to convince myself that I was just retrieving my gift from Joelle, that's all.

I tipped the tallest suitcase towards me in slow motion until it was lying flat and could be unzipped. I never realized how every little motion reverberates when you're trying to be so quiet. It seemed that the more slowly I unzipped, the louder the sound ricocheted from floor to ceiling, from wall to wall. Finally, after an excruciatingly long minute, it was open and I was greeted by the unmistakable smell of old.

There didn't seem to be anything of value here – just a bunch of notebooks with their metal spiral bindings all twisted together, and file folders with little plastic thingies for hanging, and lots and lots of yellowed newspapers. I piled everything next to me on the floor and I felt around in the zippered pockets, but there was no present there for me, so I unzipped the next suitcase, only to find more of the same – loose papers, manilla envelopes, crinkled newspaper clippings which I piled neatly on the other side of me.

Reaching for the furthest suitcase, I smelled the unmistakable smell of something else—my mother's perfume. The room grew quieter, an almost deathly quiet. I craned my head around to where the smell was coming from and there she stood in the open doorway, arms crossed stiffly in the flowered bathrobe me and my dad bought her last Mother's Day. I froze.

"You've got a lot of nerve," my mother hissed. "Do you want to tell me what you think you're doing, going through my personal belongings in the middle of the night?"

"It's actually morning," I said in the snarky voice that comes out at the most inappropriate times, especially when I'm scared. I tried to recover as quickly as I could.

"I was awake and I was just looking for my gift. I didn't look at anything of yours."

She took a step towards me as I shrank against the empty open suitcase. "Your gift! Why on earth would I have a gift for you in here, Elinor? These are special things that mean the world to me. They're all I have left of my mother. And look at them strewn all over the room!"

I caught myself before the snark came out. I didn't say, "Strewn? Look at these nice neat piles I made." Instead I whispered, "I didn't know."

"That's just it," she said. "You didn't think. You never think about the consequences, do you?"

"I'm sorry." The room felt like it was closing in. The smell of old papers mixed with her perfume was making me dizzy.

"You should be sorry, young lady. I suggest you go to your room and stay there until I calm down."

Everything seemed out of focus as I scooped up a pile of papers.

"What are you doing now? Just leave it."

I dropped what was in my hands into the open suitcase in front of me and as I moved to stand up, an image caught my eye. The newspaper that landed there on top featured a half page photo of a guy in a wheelchair. And the woman in the background looked just like Grandma Ruth.

THIRTEEN

Hide-and-Seek

I pushed past my mom in the doorway, making sure not to make eye contact, and made a blurry-eyed run to my room. Panting more heavily than necessary, I climbed into bed and pulled the covers over my head, willing myself not to cry.

Twenty-four hours ago I was waking up in Christine's room, excited about the day ahead. Now here I was lying in my own bed, head and heart filled with dread. Ah! I pulled my cell phone back out from under the pillow, sat up against the headboard, and pulled up my notes app, where I could turn my dark thoughts into a poem. My thumbs flew as I typed.

> *Waking up beside a friend*
> *Sunshine bright for the day ahead*
> *A sudden tear in the universe*

Hurls me home, sends me to bed
Heart and head replaced with rain
My day now filled with dread

And just like that, my gloom lifted. Ever since I had found poetry, I've been better at dealing with life. Well, at least most of the time. As soon as I type *my day now filled with dread*, it isn't.

I copy paste my poem into a text to Christine.

Way to make lemonade out of Miss Poet! she texted back immediately.

I'm probably grounded, I texted. But can you call me later? I'm dying to hear how it went yesterday.

I could hear the dishes clanking in the kitchen below, then the shower running, then voices in the hallway, but I couldn't make out what they were saying. A few minutes later, I heard the mechanical whine of the garage door opening, the revving of the car engine, then silence.

Utter silence.

Under my bed I had stored my stash of t-shirts from my mom's past life. I tossed on the one with the famous Spice Girl wearing her little black dress glam look, then I went tiptoeing through the house in my swirly yoga pants and '90's shirt, a PRIMA Yogarina on a mission. It ended up being Mission Impossible.

There was no sign of my parents anywhere. The car was gone and the house was empty. No note.

No sign of the suitcases either. The guest room was back to its usual sterile look – pillows fluffed and displayed like artwork on the bed, a book that's never opened on the little table next to the overstuffed chair that no one sits in, a basket of unopened toiletries and rolled up hand towels on the dresser for the guests who never visit. It was like I was seeing the room for the first time in all its loneliness.

I slowly pushed the door open to my parents' off-limits bedroom to make sure she wasn't in there lying down, but the bed was made and the blinds fully open, letting the sunshine fall across the polished floorboards. No suitcases standing beside the bed. No suitcases in the closet.

I didn't know how much time I had before they came back, so I started going room to room, looking in all the closets, behind couches, in the bathtubs, under beds. Not a suitcase to be found. It was like a one-sided game of hide-and-go-seek, and they were *not it*.

It didn't make sense. She said they were all she had left of her mother. These were her special things—was that what she said? *They mean the world to me.* Old newspapers and tattered notebooks? I couldn't stop wondering if that was really my grandmother on the front page of that paper behind the man in the wheelchair. And if it was, what was the significance? I had to find out. I headed to the garage.

When they came through the back door into the kitchen a little later, I was sitting at the table, drinking a cup of chamomile tea with honey. Indira told me that it works as a meditation enhancer, opening up your third eye. I was sipping slowly, with my eyes closed, trying to imagine where three large suitcases could be stashed. I had scoured every inch of the house and the garage.

"Well, there's our sleepyhead!" my dad announced as he plopped a box of donuts in front of me. "Let's toast the hour with some glazed goodness."

My mom handed me a juice from Nektar of the Gawds. "Pineapple passion," she said, knowing it was my absolute favorite. That's the thing with her. No I'm sorry in words, but she gets the point across. I doubt she'd even told my dad about the catastrophe in the guest room earlier.

"Is that one of the Spice Girls?" she asked eyeing my shirt. "How cute! I used to listen to them."

I thought I should tell her that I know that—that in fact this was actually her shirt, one of many hidden under my bed, but I was afraid to spoil the mood. And besides, then she might figure out that I had her high school yearbook and all those pictures of her with a boy named Curtis who looked like Manuel, the boy from Modesto who called me New Girl. Better to innocently reach into the pink box for a chocolate cake donut with sprinkles, and just nod in agreement.

"Your mom and I were at the nursery when it opened this morning," my dad said as he took a bite of a jelly donut, powdered sugar dusting his shirt. "We were thinking maybe we could have a little family bonding in the garden today. What do you say, kiddo? You in?"

Then before I could answer, he started to sing,
Yo, I'll tell you what I want, what I really really want,
So tell me what you want, what you really really want,
I wanna, I wanna, I wanna, I wanna, I wanna
really really really wanna eat another donut here with
my two best girls!

My mom did this funny little dance move that I've never seen her do before, then bumped her hip into him before pouring herself a cup of coffee in her travel mug. "Meet you both outside in ten," she said as she headed out the back door. "Just need a few minutes to center."

Sometimes I just don't get the way the world works. Adults can be so weird!

FOURTEEN

Glue

So, we spent most of the day in the garden which my mom says is good for the soul, and I guess it sort of is. When your hands are digging around in the dirt and you're helping things grow, you can't help but feel happy and calm. Our garden is huge, and we have a gardener who keeps it looking perfect, but there was still a lot to keep us busy. My dad had filled the whole back of his car with flats of bright flowers, and a delivery van from the nursery brought the rest: a little copper bird bath with a happy green frog sitting in the middle, four heart-shaped garden stones, and a beautiful blooming magnolia tree.

It took us most of the morning to transform a corner of the yard with all the new plants and things. We laid the four heart-shaped stones in a line from the gate to the new tree, then planted the flowers in a kind of heart-shape around the tree and set the birdbath off to the side.

"Time to admire our handiwork," my dad said as he stood and brushed the dirt from his knees. He had little brown rivulets of dirt running down his face, and his shirt was a filthy mess. He was humming as he stood there, waiting for me and my mom to join him. My mom brushed some of the dirt off his shirt, and said, "Are all men such little boys? Honestly, look at you!"

But she didn't say it like she usually said stuff like that. In fact, she laughed a little and then grabbed his hand.

My dad's humming turned into a melody as he sang,

And then one day you came back home. You were a creature all in rapture.

You had the key to your soul. Oh yeah, that day you came back to the garden.

I just stood there in a trance for a minute. It seemed like something important was happening. Then she reached out and grabbed my hand, too.

"You were right," she said then. "It's just perfect. And I'm sure she loves it!"

At the time I thought they meant me, but I see now that they weren't talking about me. We did all that work for Grandma Ruth. This was her garden. I just didn't know it yet.

Later that day, when Christine called me and I sat on my bed listening to her talk excitedly about meeting Liza Wren, I started to freak out a little. Well, actually more than a little. She said she was coming back to The Healing HeARTs next Saturday to watch us perform my poems. Christine and Indira had already told her all about the PRIMA Yogarinas and she told them they'd already done the hard work of coming up with the title of her next book—she loves our name. Christine said that the famous author was really cool, putting everyone at ease, and doodling little sketches in her notebook the whole time she was interviewing them.

"I can see it all so clearly," Liza Wren told Christine's mom when she was leaving. "This story is practically going to write itself. We've already got enough drama with the ballet school dropout and the carpool mom connection."

I felt my stomach drop. "What did you guys tell her about me? That sounds like I'm a weirdo or something."

Christine laughed, "Oh you are a weirdo, Elinor!"

The phone went silent. I sank back into my pillows and reached for my bluebird.

"Kidding! Geez, don't worry so much. We told her you were the reason we all came together. You're the glue. She can't wait to meet you. There's no story without you."

After we hung up, I couldn't stop thinking about what she said. *There's no story without you.*

Was that true? What if I didn't want to be in a story that told all the embarrassing details about my ballet fiasco and my obsession with writing letters to some lady in the newspaper because I was too weak to figure things out on my own? *There's no story without you.* What if I decided not to be interviewed? What if I didn't want to be a PRIMA Yogarina anymore?

What if the price of fame wasn't worth it?

tree of Life

Sunday nights are my least favorite night of the week. I always get a little sad, knowing that the weekend is over, and a little anxious—worried that I'm not prepared for the week ahead. I usually pack and unpack my backpack a few times, try on what I'm going to wear the next day, and reread my notes from the week before, adding sticky notes to the sticky notes I've already added and highlighted.

When I finished double and triple checking everything, I decided to put on some quiet music and read through my mom's high school yearbook again, looking for clues. Today I thought I saw maybe just a little glimpse of the Marsha who used to be. I scrounged around under my bed for the yearbook, flung it onto my bed, then crawled further under there to grab a t-shirt for tomorrow. Just then, a quiet rap on my door. Before

I could say, *come in,* the door swung open, and my mom and dad stood there, side-by-side, grinning. *Please, oh, please, don't tell me I'm going to be a big sister,* I thought.

As I clumsily got to my feet, I managed to toss a pillow onto the yearbook before they saw it there in all its leathery glory.

"Um, hi," I managed to squeak. "What's up?"

"We just wanted to thank you for all the help today," my mom said. "Dad told me about you missing your special day with your friend yesterday." She held out a little wrapped box. "Anyway, this is from your new little friend in Tulsa. From Grandma Ruth's funeral."

This was highly unusual. *Oh, no,* I thought. *Please don't start blubbering again.* She sniffled a little, but no tears fell.

As they both stepped all the way into the room, she handed the gift to me and pulled me into a hug, in one swift motion, something she hadn't done for a very long time. Instead of being grateful, I just felt weird. She held on for what seemed like a long time, long enough for me to glance over her shoulder and see my dad beaming like he was about to burst or something.

"Aren't you going to open it?" my dad asked, swaying back and forth to the music.

"Oh, yeah, sure," I said. I undid the wrapping. The box held a bunch of miniature rosebuds and tiny petals, pink and red, shimmery and beautiful. I thought for a minute that that was the gift, and honestly, that would have been enough. But beneath all those flowery blooms I noticed something shiny poking through. I pulled out a little bracelet made of a grass-green silky cord attached to a beautiful silver charm with a tree in the center. A shower of rose petals drifted to the floor.

"How pretty," my mom said as I slipped it on. "That's the tree of life."

"No note?" asked my dad.

"Guess not," I said, but then I noticed the teeny tiny handwritten note written inside the lid in pink gel pen.

"Returning the favor–a friendship bracelet made by hand for my *cousin,* Elinor. Twin branches of the Grandma Ruth tree."

"Cousin?" my mom stammered. "What..." But before she could say any more and ruin the moment, my dad swept in like a hero, and waltzed her toward the open door to the swelling music of the ballet coming from the speaker on my desk.

"What has gotten into you, Leo Malcolm? You're acting like a teenage boy with a crush!" She swatted at his arm, but she was smiling again. For a minute she looked like that girl wearing the Madonna t-shirt in the photos. She looked happy.

"We've kept our girl up long enough," he said to her. Then to me, "Sweet dreams, love. School tomorrow." He winked at me as he gently closed the door.

As soon as they left, I did five things.

1. I googled "tree of life" and discovered that it represented wisdom, individuality, and personal growth. I wondered if that was the message Joelle was trying to convey, or if she just liked the design and the fact that my Grandma Ruth was, as Joelle told me, a tree person. I remembered how she told me that my grandma said trees were like spirits we could commune with.

2. Next, I texted a quick message to Joelle, even though it was already late in Oklahoma, and it was a school night. Thanks, cuz. Got it. Wearing it. Love it. Within ten seconds my phone dinged back a heart emoji.

3. I opened the notes app and started a new poem. In the morning, I'd send it to Joelle.

4. And then I rescued the yearbook from beneath my pillow, climbed under the covers and studied each page from cover to cover, adding sticky notes wherever I found a possible clue to Marsha Frisbie, Class of '96.

5. I fell asleep replaying my dad's words as he left my room tonight—*sweet dreams, love* and remembering that Manuel who called me New Girl was transferring to my Spanish class tomorrow. Sweet dreams.

SIXTEEN

It's All in How You Say It

Manuel was waiting by the door to the Spanish classroom when I walked up. "Hola, Chica nueva. ¿Qué pasa?"

Swoon.

I was still just learning Spanish, but I knew enough to figure out what he said, and I could feel my face turning red. My heart did a little flip. Be cool. Be cool. Be cool, I thought.

It would be especially cool to answer in Spanish.

I quickly translated in my head, *Oh yeah? I think you're the new one! (¿Oh sí? Creo que tu eres el nuevo!")* That's what I meant to say in my best Spanish. I really did. But what came out, too loud, and right in front of the whole class as we walked through the door together was, "¿Oh sí? Creo que tu eres mi novio!" *(Oh yeah? I think you're my boyfriend!)*

Only I didn't know that's what I said. And luckily most of the other seventh graders in Spanish 1A didn't either. But Manuel must have, because then it was his turn to have his face turn red. And it was no-nonsense Ms. Lopez, who looked right at me, and said, "You may want to take the advice you're wearing and apply it to yourself. *¿Comprendes?*"

With that, everyone laughed. Everyone except me. And Manuel.

As I slunk into my seat, I felt totally confused by what had just happened. Manuel slid into the desk next to me, but he didn't say one word all class, even though he's a native Spanish speaker, and probably knew all the answers.

And he never looked at me once, even when we had to pass our papers to the left for Ms. Lopez to collect. When the bell rang at the end of class, he raced out the door before I had even packed up my backpack It wasn't until I relayed the whole thing to Christine at lunch that I understood what I'd done.

"Well, first," Christine said, "what were you trying to say? Because you just announced in front of everyone that Manuel's your boyfriend."

I nearly choked on my tater tot. "No, I didn't. He called me New Girl again so I just said he's the new one. And he is. I've been here my whole life and he just moved here."

"Well, I think you were trying to say *nuevo*, but it sounds like you said *novio* instead. Boyfriend."

My lunch suddenly felt like lead inside me.

"So, I guess Lopez was trying to be funny when she told you to take the advice you're wearing."

"I don't get it."

Christine sounded exasperated. "Maybe if she'd said *who* you're wearing, you'd have caught on quicker."

And then all the puzzle pieces came together at once, in one big embarrassing jolt. Gwen Stefani. My mom's '90s t-shirt that she wore in high school. It looked so cool this morning when I put it on, and sort of ironic. I thought it would be like a conversation piece, with girls asking me where I got it, and what it meant.

But Ms. Lopez was right. Good advice, just a little late. Now I'd ruined everything. Manuel would probably hate me forever. I'll never have a boyfriend. Not cool. Eli-not-normal strikes again.

SEVENTEEN

Tea and Sympathy

After school, Christine and I were supposed to have a google hangout session, but I texted and said I didn't feel well. That was not a lie. And the next morning I told my mom that I had a pounding headache and would have to stay home.

She felt my head, and said, "No fever. No glassy eyes. No runny nose. I'd say you're fine."

"I don't feel fine though," I said. "And you know I never miss school. But my head is killing me. Really."

She must have still been in a good mood from our Sunday bonding session in the garden though, because she immediately relented. "Try to go back to sleep and I'll call the school. And I'll bring you up a cup of tea and some crackers in a little bit. Tea and sleep are the best medicine there is—you'll be as good as new by this afternoon. Guaranteed." Then she kissed me on the forehead.

A cup of tea and a kiss on the forehead is something my dad would do. It's probably something Mrs. Corrales would do. It's definitely something Indira's mom would do. But my mother? This was way out of character. I pulled the covers over my head and tried to sort things out.

Instead of falling back to sleep, I just lay there imagining what was going on at school. Had the news gotten out that I'd made a fool of myself over the first boy I've ever had a crush on? I kept picturing how red his face had gotten and how quickly he'd dashed out of the classroom yesterday. He looked so embarrassed, thinking that someone as dorky as me could be his girlfriend. I'd ruined everything. From now on I'd be Weird Girl instead of New Girl.

Last year I would have written to Carpool Mom to pour out my troubles and ask her advice. But I had a mom. And she was right downstairs, making me tea. She'd kissed me on the forehead. She'd planted a garden with me. She was a different mom than the one who'd dragged me through the airport a few weeks ago.

I got out of bed, and headed downstairs. In the kitchen, a mug of no-longer hot tea in my special *brew-tea-ful* mug sat on a tray on the counter alongside a bowl of those little oyster crackers. Mom's miracle cure for headaches and heartaches. But my mom was nowhere to be found.

The house was silent. I looked in all the downstairs rooms, then I followed a muddy trail from the backdoor up the back steps to my mom's office. The door was cracked open a little bit, so I pushed it in all the way. At first I thought her office was empty too, then I saw her foot sticking out from behind her thinking sofa.

"Mom?" I took a hesitant step further into the room.

Her head popped up. "Elinor? What on earth?"

"I didn't know where you were. I thought maybe something…"

"Oh, for pity's sake!" She stood up, brushing herself off, and came around to face me. "You and that imagination of yours. What on earth could have happened to me in my own house?"

I didn't tell her all the awful things that had run through my head in the course of just a few minutes. Coyote attack. Heart attack. Abduction. Murder. She's right—I do have an unhealthy imagination sometimes.

"Well, I said, "it's just that my tea was cold and I couldn't find you and the stairs were all muddy and…" I stepped forward in relief to give her a hug, but she backed up at the same time, then looked down at her muddy feet.

"Oh dear." As she bent down to inspect her slippers, I made a startling discovery.

On the floor behind the sofa was an open suitcase, its contents spilled all over the carpet. Photographs. Newspapers. Folders. Letters. And staring right up at me was that front page article starring a man in a wheelchair and what looked like the ghost of my Grandma Ruth.

EIGHTEEN

Lovemore

So there I was in limbo. Forever to be known as the weird girl at school and the drama queen at home. I just wanted to be normal. And now on top of everything, I realized I was missing the most important day of yearbook, the day when all the assignments and offices were going to be up for grabs. I'd be stuck with whatever the worst job was. My partner would probably end up being that little sixth grader, McHenry Plouffe and Christine would get partnered up with one of the band girls. My weirdness cemented for the rest of my life.

I had two choices, it seemed. I could either climb back into bed and continue pretending to be sick, or I could get dressed and ask my mother to drive me to school so I wouldn't miss the whole day, now that my headache had "miraculously" disappeared.

But option B was not to be. "I am up to my eyeballs in work," she told me. "And headaches don't just go poof like that. Go heat up your tea and then get back in that bed. And close the door on the way out."

I pulled out my *Before She Was Mom* journal, and started a new page. At the top I wrote: Unanswered Questions, News, and Clues.

Where's she been hiding that suitcase full of old junk?

Why is my meticulous mom wearing muddy slippers?

What kind of "work" is she up to her eyeballs in?

Who is that man in the wheelchair?

Was that my grandma's ghost?

What is my mother up to?

Who is Marsha Frisbie?

And then I developed a headache for real. I pulled the covers back over my head and fell into a fitful sleep.

The next day I wore my tree of life bracelet and my bravest face. When I got off the bus, I headed straight to my group, holding my head up high. Brit spoke first. "How was your date?"

Then Sasha chimed in, singing, "Ellie and Manny sitting in a tree." I looked around at everyone winking at me and making kissy faces. Even Christine said, "Details, details. Give us the scoop."

"What are you guys talking about?" I tried to say it in my calmest voice.

Lucy, the other band girl said, "You and Manny. Both absent on the same day. Like did you meet up?"

I sputtered.

"Or did you just spend the whole day texting with an S if you get my drift?"

This was too much! I couldn't even answer, just stormed off into the building and ran straight into Ms. Loveless carrying a jumble of papers that spilled haphazardly onto the floor as I skidded to a stop.

"Good grief! Where are you going in such a hurry? You almost trampled me to death!"

I bent over to help her pick up the scattered quizzes. "Good, you can help me re-alphabetize these," she said as she headed toward homeroom, me trailing behind with a messy stack. "Okay, partner?"

Partner?

She unlocked the door and flicked on the lights as more papers drifted to the linoleum. I rescued the rest and then helped her spread them out across the front counter.

"Actually," she said as I began gathering up the A's and B's, "can you take care of this while I go pick up the mail from my mailbox? I didn't have a chance to run by the office yet today. Oh, and it's last name first." She was out the door before I could even answer, and a minute later the bell rang.

So, there I was, standing front and center in the teacher's spot when my noisy classmates entered the room.

There are times when you want everybody to notice you. And then there are times like this. All eyes were on me. I wished I could just disappear.

"Are you going to take attendance?" someone called out. "Oh, never mind. I thought you were Loveless."

And then from the back of the room, "Nope. I think that must be Lovemore!" A cascade of laughter followed, as Ms. Loveless re-entered the room and restored order. I slunk into my seat and waited for the bell.

I hung out in the library during lunch and I was going to text Indira to share my troubles with her, but I knew she'd say, "You know what to do." She always says if you look inside, you can find the answers. But I really didn't know what to do. My insides were all jumbled up. Even

Christine thought I had skipped school with Manuel. How could she think that?

I thought maybe I could text Joelle since she didn't know any of the people involved and could be objective. I hid my phone inside a book I pulled from the nearest shelf, and composed a message.

Sitting alone in the library.

Stuck inside my own head.

The boy I like thinks I'm a weird new girl.

My best friend...

But then I couldn't think what else to say. Was Christine still my best friend? What about Indira?

I twirled my tree of life bracelet and thought about Grandma Ruth. She was my connection to Joelle and Joelle was my connection to my mother's past. Maybe.

I copied what I'd written so far and pasted it in my future poems file. Then I started over.

Hey, Joelle.

What do you know about a guy in a wheelchair?

Just wondering.

NINETEEN

Loveless

In Spanish class, when Manuel slid into the desk next to me, somebody said, "Oooh!" but Ms. Lopez shot one of those killer teacher's looks and the room fell silent. I scribbled a quick "sorry" on my notebook page and turned it towards Manuel. He didn't say anything, but his pencil started moving feverishly across his notebook. I was trying to pay attention to the teacher, but I kept stealing looks at his desk trying to see what he was working on so furiously.

Then Ms. Lopez announced that we'd be working on our dialogues, and I got paired up with the girl who sits in front of me. Manuel moved to the back of the room to work with somebody else, taking his notebook with him.

When the bell rang, as I was gathering up my notes, I heard a little cough behind me—one of those little throat-clearing coughs you do when you're trying to get someone's attention. A piece of notebook paper folded up into a tiny little square landed on my desk. Probably a cease-and-desist letter. I shoved it in my pocket and headed for the restroom so I could cry in peace.

I locked myself in a stall and slowly unfolded the paper, taking deep cleansing breaths like Indira taught me. I could hear Indira's voice in my head whispering, *center, center.* There was no note. No writing. Just a very, very detailed drawing. Of me.

Heading toward the parking lot, Christine ran up beside me, breathless. "Guess what? I got picked to stay after for band rehearsal. I get a solo!"

She acted like everything was normal between us.

I kept walking toward the bus.

"So, I can't come over today." I had forgotten that I had invited her. "But tomorrow, okay?" She had to kind of shout that last part as a swarm of sixth graders came flying out of the multi-purpose room.

We got separated by the rush of kids pushing their way past me onto the bus. This is something I will never understand. The bus won't leave without us. There's enough room for everyone. But, like, everybody wants to be first. Every day. Especially the sixth graders who all move together in one big clump.

I had to stand on my tiptoes to see Christine while managing to not get trampled. She was still grinning from ear to ear.

We must still be friends. "Okay, I guess," I shouted over the crowd. "Tomorrow!"

As I was stepping onto the noisy bus, I turned around to say, "Oh, and congratulations!" but Christine had disappeared back into the building. I was the last one onto the bus and there was only one empty seat. McHenry Plouffe.

He patted the seat next to him. I had no choice.

"Your lucky day!" he said. He's very sure of himself for a weird little sixth grader.

I readjusted my backpack on my lap and pulled out a book. This is my go-to on public transportation. Nose in a book usually means that no one engages you in pointless conversation. But he was not no one.

"What are you reading?" I turned the book towards him so he could see, then flipped to the page with my bookmark.

"Oh cool! I'm a big reader too. I've read all the Peak Marcello books and Maze Runner and Divergent and…" He listed another dozen series titles, as I tried to tune him out and figure out the meaning behind the picture Manuel drew of me. I kept my eyes glued to the open book balanced on my backpack. McHenry did not take the hint.

"So, you missed yearbook yesterday."

Oh, no. In all the Manuel drama I forgot to ask Christine if we chose partners.

"Guess who your partner is!"

I closed my book. This day could not get any stranger. Dating rumors. Lovemore label. Pencil portrait. I let out a long sigh. McHenry was sitting beside me in his neon shorts and puppy polo shirt. I noticed his scraped knees and mismatched socks. He was drumming with two pencils on his orange camo backpack.

"You'll never guess, Elinor. In a million years."

I was so annoyed by this time. "I think it's pretty obvious it's you." I shoved my book back into my backpack as the bus screeched to a stop. "And isn't this your neighborhood?"

"I can get off at the next stop," he said, then resumed his drumming. "And, nope, not me. Drumroll, please!"

Well then who on earth could it be? Who would I be stuck with? Surely not one of the other band girls. They would definitely all be partnered up.

"It's Loveless."

The bus fell silent just at the moment he said it, the words hanging in the air. I fell completely silent too, my mouth opening and closing like a fish gasping for air. Why did partnering with McHenry Plouffe now seem like it would have been the best option after all?

He stood up then and pushed/climbed his way over me. "There was an odd number, so she said 'Well, I guess I'm on New Girl's team.'" With that he tried to high five me but missed and smacked my shoulder when the bus lurched. "Sorry, Elinor. Gotta go!"

TWENTY

Puzzle Pieces

As soon as I got home, I unfolded Manuel's drawing again. I smoothed out the wrinkles with my hand and studied it. The girl in the sketch was not smiling, but it was definitely me. She was even wearing my butterfly earrings. And something I hadn't noticed before. A skinny little bracelet circling her left wrist. It's hard to see the detail because it's so small, but I think the tree of life is in the center.

So, Manuel is more than just a cute boy with a killer dimple and dark eyes flecked with gold.

He's an observer.

He's an artist.

He's a mystery.

Was this drawing his answer to my hastily scribbled *I'm sorry?*

Does this mean he forgives me for embarrassing him?

Does this mean he likes me back?

I took out my phone to take a photo of the sketch. Maybe Indira would be able to read between the lines and tell me what it meant. She's had way more experience with love than I have, especially since I've had exactly zero experience.

My phone was dead. That would explain why Joelle hadn't texted me back yet. I plugged in the charger and the screen sprang to life.

Nope. But I'm on it. Joelle.

Working late. Don't wait up. Mom

Yogarina Update. Indira

Wrenterview. Indira

Knock, knock. Indira

You there? Indira

I texted Joelle back first. I told her about the picture in the newspaper. She said that was a great clue and she'd start digging. I told her I missed her and she texted back a smiley face. I wish people would say what they mean instead of sharing emojis or hashtags. Or instead of drawing mysterious pictures that keep you guessing.

I texted Indira to get an actual translation of her message. Turns out Liza Wren got the go-ahead from her publisher and is working on an outline for the book.

Indira told her I'd be available for an in-depth in-person interview on Saturday. I didn't tell Indira that I didn't want to be part of the story anymore. I never can say no to her but I still had a few days to think of a way to get out of it. I didn't send her the photo of my Manuel sketch like I'd planned to either. Maybe it was time to keep a special secret of my very own.

And last I texted my mom. She texted back that she was driving my dad to the airport, then heading back to the office for a late-night session with the legal team. I didn't even know my dad was off on another business trip. This time he was going to Japan for two weeks. How did I not know that? I didn't even give him a hug goodbye this time. "He didn't want to wake you," she texted. "He left you a note."

I changed into my running shoes and headed out for a long walk to clear my head. It felt like all the weird stuff happening around me were clues to be solved, like pieces of a jigsaw puzzle dumped at my feet by the universe. I just had to put them all together to figure it out. "You know what to do." Indira's voice in my head again. I wished I did.

I walked for a long time, but my head was not any clearer. Thoughts and memories were swirling around faster and faster, bumping and colliding. Prima Yogarinas. The Healing HeARTs. Lovemore.

Loveless. Grandma Ruth. Missing suitcases. Muddy slippers. Wheelchair man. Tree of Life. Everything was connected. But how?

When I got home from my walk, I searched the house again for those suitcases that could be the key to solving the mystery that was Marsha Frisbie Malcolm. They had to be here somewhere.

My mother always says, "a place for everything and everything in its place," and she's not kidding. My house is the most organized place you've ever seen. I started my search in her office. That's where I had seen the open suitcase behind the thinking sofa yesterday, but there was no trace of it now. Gone. The muddy tracks were gone. The top of her desk was completely cleared off, the books and files all lined up by height and color along the shelves. Every room throughout the house was the same. Neat and clean and organized—nothing out of place, nothing out of order.

I needed a place to think. I grabbed my journal and headed for the garden, to the spot where we had all worked together on Sunday. Here we were a normal, happy family weeding and digging and laughing and singing. Just the three of us.

I sat under the little magnolia tree that I had helped plant, and started a sketch. Then a poem came to me. A tribute to my Grandma Ruth.

In the garden
We notice life
A tree, a blossom, a buzzing bee
We are all connected
to each other, across the days,
across the years, across forever

And then I had a brilliant idea. This peaceful spot should have a poetry walk. I could make it as a surprise for my mom. A memorial garden for remembering Grandma Ruth.

When Christine came over after school tomorrow, I'd share my idea with her and she could help me design and build it. Just the kind of creative project we loved to collaborate on. Art. Nature. Words. Just the kind of creative outlet I needed to help me deal with the chaos in my life. Words. Nature. Art. And the perfect way to tell her that I had changed my mind—I can't be part of a story that shows the world what a weirdo I am.

The temperature dropped as the sun started to set, so I stood up and brushed the dirt from my yoga pants. Yoga. That's when it hit me. Could I still be one of the Prima Yogarinas if I wasn't part of Liza Wren's book? Why did everything have to be so complicated?

As I headed back to the house, I heard a blast from the past coming from the very back of the yard. I hadn't heard that sound in forever, but it was unmistakable.

Woodpecker. Flashback to the first time I heard one in the trees at Grandma Ruth's house. I must have been five or six. I was with my mom and dad, sitting in these painted wooden chairs on her deck while Grandma Ruth was inside cooking. I remember being scared at first and asking my dad what that sound was. "That, my dear, is the sound of opportunity knocking!"

Tap tap tap. I followed the sound. It was coming from behind the shed. Tap. Tap. Tap. I looked up in the treetops, but it was not coming from that direction. It was coming from the shed! A red-headed bird was pounding away where the back wall met the roof. Weird, I thought. Weird but cool.

I stood watching for a minute longer. It felt like the woodpecker resented my presence, as he stopped tapping and just stayed silent, attached to the side of the shed, defying gravity. "Okay," I said out loud. "I'll give you your privacy, bird!" I turned around, and there on the path behind me, sticking out from underneath the bushes, a red handle. I bent down to pick it up, only to discover it was one of my dad's hammers. *Hmmm…that's weird,* I thought. My dad is so particular about his tools. I couldn't imagine him ever leaving one outside on the ground. Maybe it was the gardener.

My dad would probably understand, but I knew if my mom found out, Martin would be fired for sure. I picked it up and walked around to the front of the shed. There was a shiny new padlock on the door. How strange. Another puzzle piece dropped from the sky.

TWENTY-ONE

Sayonara

he next morning, the house was empty when I got up, but my mom had obviously been home because there were two notes waiting for me on the kitchen table when I came downstairs for breakfast. The one on top was from my mom on her Marsha Malcolm, Attorney at Law notepaper. *Trial starting. Long day. Home late again. Mom.* Underneath that was a sealed envelope addressed to Ellie-Bear in my dad's familiar handwriting. There was a heart over the i, like always. I opened it slowly.

So sorry I missed you, bug, but I had to catch an early flight. Two weeks will fly by. Let's have a movie marathon when I get back—there's a cool Japanese love story about a girl in middle school who turns into a cat that I want to share with you. Don't worry—there are subtitles so you won't have to listen to my sorry translation! Anyway, big time difference but I'll set up a FaceTime session or two with you, and then I'll be home. Take good care of your mom for me. Love you to a galaxy far, far away and back. Daddy-o.

I folded the note back neatly and tucked it inside the envelope, before transferring it to the pocket of my backpack so I could read it again and again. Then I grabbed a breakfast bar, made sure I had enough money for lunch, turned off the lights, and headed for the bus.

I couldn't wait till the next yearbook day to find out what was up with Ms. Loveless being my partner. I couldn't even imagine what that meant. Who ever heard of a kid having to partner up with a teacher on a project? I hopped off the bus and went around the back of the building to avoid Christine and the band girls standing in their usual spot under the gym overhang.

It had never occurred to me that other people would be hanging out back waiting for the bell, too. As I rounded the side of the building, I had to skirt around a group of boys who must have been in 8th grade and they were all wearing ties which if you ask me, is pretty weird in middle school. There was another small clump of kids all working in their notebooks together, and along the back wall there was one kid sitting all alone on the blacktop, nose buried in a book. McHenry Plouffe. He didn't look up as I hurried by.

I opened the back door quickly and darted inside before anyone saw me. I had five minutes before the bell rang, and I hoped that I'd find Ms. Loveless in homeroom, getting ready for the day. She was sitting on top of the front counter with her headphones on, humming. She had her eyes closed and didn't feel my presence there, so I gently tapped her arm.

"Good gravy! You nearly gave me a coronary!"

I backed away a little. "I'm sorry, I…"

She didn't even let me get the rest out. "Never mind. Here to sort papers for me again?"

"No, I…"

She handed me a stack from beside her. "Last name first."

I didn't have much time before the crush of kids entered and the school day started. "No, I wasn't in yearbook the other day. I was sick, and…"

She jumped off the counter and slipped into her ugly shoes that were under a front row desk as she stuffed her headphones into a drawer. "Ah, yearbook. And your point is?" She tapped the top sheet of the stack of papers in front of me where *Erik Acosta* was printed in the top-right hand corner above the date. "Pay attention, partner. Start with Aboudi."

Partner? There it was again. Partner. It proved to be nearly impossible to alphabetize and think and talk all at the same time. I flipped through the stack until I found Mary Aboudi, then moved her paper to the top. At this rate, I'd never finish.

"Sit at my desk and finish up while I take roll," she said as the bell rang. In another few seconds, homeroom would start. I had missed my chance.

At lunch Christine could talk about nothing but her solo coming up in the fall band concert next month. She was so excited that I couldn't get a word in edgewise. Then she said that she'd probably have to skip going to The Healing HeARTs for the next several Saturdays since she was going to have extra band practices until her debut as a solo artist. "But you can go without me and work on the choreography with Indira, right? We can still be the Prima Yogarinas and you can just teach me what I miss."

"What about our book deal?" I felt a sense of impending doom kick in.

Now that Christine wouldn't be going, that meant her mom wouldn't be driving us there which meant I wouldn't be meeting Liza Wren. And even though I said I didn't want to be in a book before, and I was trying to figure out a way to get out of it, now that it looked like that option was gone, I desperately wanted to get there. I desperately wanted to tell my story to someone in my own words.

Christine looked shocked. "Why do you look so mad? We already gave her plenty of material to get started." She broke her chocolate bar in half and passed me a piece without missing a beat. "And Indira and I worked on our performance when you weren't there, so I don't see what the big deal is if I miss a few. You guys are the creative geniuses anyway. You've got all those cool poems, and she's got all those amazing yoga dance moves. You guys can collaborate and then loop me in." She zipped her reusable containers and bamboo fork back into her lunch bag and stood up. "Gotta get my flute out of my locker before the bell rings. I'll catch you later."

And with that she was gone. She hadn't given me a chance to tell her there was no way I could get there Saturday if her mom didn't drive me. She didn't give me a chance to find out how I got stuck with Loveless on yearbook and what that meant. And worst of all, she was so wrapped up in her solo that she forgot she was supposed to be coming over after school today. On my own again.

TWENTY-TWO

Eureka!

This day will go down in the annals of Elinor Malcolm's history as a human being. I made about a million discoveries in the space of one amazing afternoon. First of all, Christine, came chasing after me, swinging her flute by her side as I left the cafeteria alone. "Oh, my gosh, Elinor, I completely forgot! I have to watch the boys after school today." She grabbed my arm and we both stood there looking at each other. "I'm such a dodo bird," she said in apology. I felt a wave of calm pass over me, as she continued to hold onto my arm. "Still besties?"

I have to stop jumping to conclusions. I have to start having more faith in people. "Absolutely!" I said. "My bestie is a famous musician." And then it hit me— the perfect way to up our game and make us all equal partners in the PRIMA Yogarinas. "Can you maybe play your flute for our performance?"

"Wow, you are brilliant, Elinor. Simply brilliant. The poet, the dancer, and the flutist!"

And then we both shouted, "Three Prima Yogarinas!" at the same time just as the bell rang and we dashed down the hall laughing, oblivious to all those kids looking at us like we were crazy.

Discovery number two happened when I skidded into Spanish and Manuel was already at his desk next to mine. "Ola, Chica," he said out loud, flashing that impressive dimpled smile. I thought my heart would explode. And then as I slid, red-faced, into my seat, he whispered, in English, "Cool shirt." I looked down at what I was wearing. Just a plain white top. No '90's rock stars. No naughty sayings. Just me. Plain old me.

When I looked back up, he was staring at me with those gold-flecked movie star eyes. He pointed at me then and said nearly under his breath, but not quite, *"bonita."* That was one of this week's vocabulary words. *Pretty.* Did he mean my shirt?

Or me?

Or was he just practicing his vocab?

Doesn't matter any way, I'll take it!

Manuel Garcia said *bonita.* To me.

Discovery number three happened on the bus going

home today. I actually chose to sit next to McHenry. I guess I felt sort of sorry for him when I saw him sitting all alone reading against the building this morning before school. A weird little friendless sixth grader. I could definitely relate. Before I had a chance to start up a conversation and maybe find out more about the yearbook assignments he blurted, "Why were you going in the back door this morning?"

"No reason," I said. "Just checking out the scenery. I didn't see you." (Little white lie). I was trying to save him from the embarrassment of being discovered all alone like that, sitting along the wall like I used to do.

"I always go in that way," he announced cheerily. I guess he didn't mind being a loner. "I like to read before school. Well, read and people-watch."

He told me that he hangs out there during lunch too. He said one of the guidance counselors called his parents about it but he told them that he's not anti-social, he's just a reader. And then he told me about the 8th grade boys in their ties. "You know how Mr. F is the basketball coach, right?" I nodded. "Well, you know how he always wears a tie?" Another nod. "So, I guess he told his team that he'd give them all extra scrimmage time if they dressed like gentlemen. I'm going to interview them for the school newspaper."

"You're on newspaper, too? Not just yearbook?" I had to grab the seat in front of me as the bus lurched forward.

"Just for my Language Arts class. We don't have a school newspaper, you know." He turned to me with the most serious face, then broke into a huge grin. "Yet!"

This kid was just full of surprises and ideas for a little sixth grader. A school newspaper!

I'm sure he could sense my excitement at the prospect. "And, Elinor, I bet we could get old Loveless to help us get it started."

This time when he high-fived me, he didn't miss.

You would think that would be enough discoveries for one person for one day, but the biggest, most surprising discovery of all awaited me when I got home.

One of my mom's Marsha Malcolm, Attorney at Law notes was attached by a magnet to the side of the refrigerator. It had only one thing written on it: 10-13-78. My mother's birthday. *That's weird,* I thought. *Why would my mom have to write down her own birthday? It's not like that's something a person ever forgets.*

I stood there, transfixed for a moment, thinking. Indira's voice in my head again. *The answer is inside you.* And suddenly it was. I left my backpack on the floor and rushed outside into the back yard.

TWENTY-THREE

Click

I darted across the lawn, still wet from the sprinklers, and dashed behind the shed, retrieving the red-handled hammer that I'd re-hidden beneath the bushes. It felt heavier in my hand than yesterday. Maybe because of what I was about to do.

Swinging it by my side, I scurried along the back of the shed, peered around the corner to make sure I was alone, then skidded to a stop at the padlocked door. I told myself I was just going to open the door, hang the hammer in its proper place along my dad's workbench, and then go back in the house and start my homework. But all the while I knew that wasn't true. That's not why I was there.

I dropped the hammer to the ground. Then, hands shaking, turned the dial. 10-13-78. Nothing happened.

Once more. Nothing. *Center, center,* I told myself. This time I took a deep cleansing breath and concentrated, turning it clockwise, slowly past the zero. Ten. Back the other way, slowly. Thirteen. Then clockwise again, so slowly. Painfully slowly, my eyes focused like lasers on the dial, my ears cocked and listening for the magic click. Seventy-eight. Click. The shackle slid out. The lock was unlocked. The door swung open.

It took a minute for my eyes to adjust. The windowless shed was eerily dark inside and had an overpowering smell of something gross. Death? That was my first thought and it almost made me lose my nerve. "This is just my dad's tool shed," I said out loud to the lawnmower, gripping the handle to steady myself. I took some more centering breaths, waited for my eyes to adjust, and then, of course, there they were—two brand new black suitcases from my mom's trip home from Tulsa.

My heart was flip-flopping in my chest. Why were the suitcases out here? What secrets must they be hiding? I was about to find out. I tiptoed back to the door and closed it tight, felt my way across the shed, and knelt in front of the closest suitcase. I could hear the blood rushing in my ears. *Breathe. Breathe.* I turned it on its side to unzip it, telling myself that I was just looking for mementos from my Grandma Ruth. That's all.

The zipper was closed with a little lock that you open with a key. I grabbed the other suitcase and laid it on its side beside the first one. Another lock. Another challenge. Another piece of the still unsolved puzzle.

I spent the rest of the afternoon searching for the keys—a spy in my own home—tiptoeing from room to room, silently sliding open off-limits drawers and cabinets. The combination had been hidden in plain sight. So where could the missing keys be?

And then I remembered something. In science, we were studying the engineering standards and Janna Faz was my partner for the simple machines' unit. She told me how she picked the lock on her older sister's diary, and then she showed me the tool she used which was just a bent paper clip. At the time I remember thinking, why would anyone still keep a diary when you could just use the notes app on your phone, but I didn't say that. She tried to explain the science behind it, but to tell you the truth, I wasn't really listening to her. I was picturing what it would be like to have an older sister. Kind of like Indira.

I pulled out my phone and googled *how to pick a lock with a paperclip,* and there, just like Janna described, was a step-by-step tutorial. I opened the junk drawer in the kitchen and dug around through the ketchup packets and batteries and rubber bands and matches and receipts. Not one paper clip. But something even better! There, taped to the inside of the drawer, hiding in plain sight, a little silver ring with two tiny silver keys attached.

I slipped the keys into my pocket and opened the back door just I heard the garage door going up.

"Surprise! We recessed early after all so I picked up dinner!" My mom came bounding through the back door. She dropped a takeout bag on the counter. "Homework all finished?"

"Yup. Almost. Just came in here for a drink." I filled a glass with water from the fridge and guzzled it so I could make the lie be true.

"Well, I must say," she said, "this was an exceptionally good day. I'm planning to have a nice hot soak, watch some reality TV and just hang out. Care to join me?"

I refilled the glass and took another long swig. All I could think about were the keys in my pocket, the unlocked shed, and those mysterious suitcases calling my name.

The evening dragged on and I must say I wasn't very good company. Here I was, finally getting a chance to have some together time with my always too-busy mom, and all I could think about was how to escape. I hadn't done any homework, I had a poem running through my head that I was dying to write, and I had to get back outside to the shed before it was too late. But here I was watching some lame show about a model who wants to marry the wrong guy. "She's going to regret that," my mom said. "Believe me. That guy is a rake."

I had no idea what she meant, but that made me wonder. Was there a wrong guy in her life? She couldn't possibly mean my dad! I wished I could ask her. I shifted closer to her on the sofa and took a stab at it. "What do you mean? Like how do you know who's the wrong guy?"

"Trust me, Elinor. The pretty boys are just the worst. They break your heart."

The guy in her yearbook? Was he a pretty boy? Did he break her heart?

Did you ever want to ask somebody a question but you were afraid of what the answer might be?

We watched the rest of the show in silence, then I finally feigned a yawn and said I was going to get ready for bed. She stood up at the same time and gave me a hug. A real hug. "This was nice, Elinor," she said with her arms wrapped around me tight. "Thanks for hanging out. And goodness, gracious–you're almost as tall as me now." She kissed the top of my head and looked into my eyes before letting go. "And remember, beware of those pretty boys."

I walked upstairs in a daze, picturing Manuel with his dimple and his gold-flecked eyes, and the way he whispered *bonita*. I still had to do my math homework, I had to read that chapter on traveling to the moon in the engineering section of my science textbook, I had to write that poem that was dancing in my heart, and I had to head back out to the shed once my mom's light went off and at least lock the door. I didn't think I was brave enough to work out there in the pitch dark. Then I had to tape these keys back in the kitchen drawer without anyone being the wiser.

But all I wanted to do was fall asleep and dream about Manuel. I took the picture he drew of me out of my backpack and stared into my own eyes. Bonita. New Girl. Elinormal. It was going to be a very long night.

TWENTY-FOUR

All the News that's Fit to Print

I woke up the next morning to a text from Joelle.

Serendipity–do–da!

Call me.

ASAP

She answered on the first ring, and didn't even say hello, just launched right into her news.

"So, you know how I love to sit under that tree at the park and listen to the wind?" I was nodding and picturing that beautiful old oak where we first shared a friendship bracelet made from blades of grass.

"Well, yesterday I went there after school to decompress and I could have sworn I heard your Grandma Ruth's voice. It sounded like she was calling my name. I got goosebumps."

Something told me this news was going to be a big deal. Definitely one of those messages from the universe. My arms were covered in goosebumps too. I sat up straighter, twirled my tree of life bracelet, and pressed the phone closer.

"And there," she continued, "right in front of me on the path was a guy in a wheelchair."

Serious goosebumps. "Was it him?"

"That's what I'm getting at," she said. "I said 'Excuse me, sir. I'm a student reporter for my school newspaper' and asked him if he'd be willing to answer a few questions."

"Oh my gosh, Joelle. You're amazing. What did he say?"

"Well, he was a talker, that's for sure. He practically told me his whole life story."

"And was it him?"

It was taking her a very long time to get to the point. She told me how she ended up talking to him for a half an hour and finally managed to get around to asking if he knew a lady named Ruth Frisbie who had just died. "Hmmm," he said. "Sort of sounds familiar, so might've heard of her, but never met the lady. She famous?"

My head was spinning by that time so I might have missed some of what she said next, but then she told me that he said he plays wheelchair basketball with a bunch of guys every weekend. He said he could ask around.

"So maybe he knows him then? But how will he let you know?" I had a million questions racing through my head.

Joelle said he told her that if she was at the park next week to look for him and he could tell her if any of the guys knew a Miss Frisbie. He also said, "I'm kind of easy to spot, and I'm here every day at this time getting my exercise."

Every day. That means that he's been there every time Joelle goes there after school to sit under the tree. He was probably there when I was there with Joelle last month too. This is the kind of stuff that just kills me. Somebody tells you the meaning of a word you've never heard before, and then you see and hear it everywhere. Someone tells you they're looking for a guy in a wheelchair, and there he is, right in front of you. The strange thing is, he's always been there. You just couldn't see him before. Weird.

By the time we hung up, I was running late for school. I threw my hair up into a messy bun, pulled on a denim skirt, and didn't even change the shirt I'd slept in last night. I guess a wrinkled *Isn't it Ironic* t-shirt would have to do.

TWENTY-FIVE

Irony

It was hard to concentrate in school with all the drama playing out in my life. Joelle was on the trail of the wheelchair guy. There were two locked suitcases in the shed and two silver keys to open them taped inside a kitchen drawer. My mom said to beware of pretty boys who break girls' hearts. My hair was a mess and I was wearing my pajama shirt. That unwritten poem was still jangling around in my head and even though I had read the science chapter I hadn't *really* read it because I couldn't remember any of the details. Like I said, drama!

Then, to top it all off, Loveless called me partner again, so I hung around after homeroom and asked her what I was supposed to be doing for yearbook. "Well, isn't that ironic?" she said and then launched into one of her laughing snorts.

I didn't think it was funny.

"You've actually been doing it already," she said. "Your yearbook assignment is to help keep me organized. The paper sorting's been super helpful."

"I don't get it," I said. "What does alphabetizing math homework and quizzes have to do with working on the yearbook?" I might have sounded a little snippy.

"Oh, my dear girl, it has everything to do with it. That's a real time saver for me—with your help I can just enter grades one-two-three, lickety split. You know the advanced math parents want to know what their kid's grade is every day. If I don't post those grades by the end of day, they'll have my head."

I was trying to follow.

"And if that happens, no more yearbook. It's all connected, see?"

"But I want to work on the actual yearbook. Like, for real."

"Tell you what," she said as her first period brainiacs came through the door. "Think about what kind of changes you think we could make to this year's book to make it unique. Really think about it. And at next Tuesday's meeting you and I can work out a plan to do just that and present it to the team. Deal?"

I was still not convinced or very happy about teaming up with the most unpopular teacher at school, but I didn't want to have the yearbook disappear either. "Deal," I said as I headed out the door to the sound of the late bell.

The hallway was eerily quiet and completely empty and I realized there was no way Mr. Hoy would let me come into history even one minute late without a pass, even if I'd been with a teacher. I headed to the office.

The lady standing at the counter seemed a bit grumpy when I walked in, and gave me a look. "Late pass?"

"Yeah," I said. "I was talking to my homeroom teacher."

"Well, you should have asked them for a pass then."

I hate when people have to go and make things so complicated.

When I didn't answer, she slapped a pack of late passes on the counter, and ripped off the top one. "Name?"

"Ms. Loveless."

"Oh, my word," she said sounding completely frustrated at this intrusion on her time doing whatever the ladies in the office do when they're not writing out late passes. "Not her name. Yours!"

I told her my name but she reacted the same way Indira did the first time she heard it. "Elinormal what?"

And before I could repeat it and correct her, she looked up with a smirk. The office door had opened behind me with a whoosh. "Ah, late again, Mr. Garcia. And what's the excuse this time?"

That's when the air in the room shifted, and like magic, Manuel Garcia was standing next to me at the counter.

the Plot thickens

Christine couldn't believe it when I found her at lunch. I told her everything that was happening in my life, starting with the fact that Manuel winked at me and said, "Hey, Chica" when he looked up and realized we were both late for school except I really wasn't, I just was talking to Ms. Loveless for too long and then the late bell rang. He was actually late because he missed the bus which sounded like something that happened a lot.

"I think he's trouble," Christine said. "He just can get away with things 'cause he's so cute. Let's just hope nobody saw the two of you coming out of the office together with those late passes."

"He is cute," I said, my face turning red. "And I think, maybe, he likes me."

"Well, watch out, that's all I'm saying."

We sat in silence for a bit while I sucked on my water bottle. Then Christine passed me a homemade chocolate chip cookie and said, "Well, what else? You said you had a lot to tell me."

So, I rattled off all the other things going on—the suitcases, and the hidden keys, and the wheelchair guy for starters.

"Wowzers," she said. "You're going to be the main character in Liza Wren's book, for sure. Your whole life is one big drama."

Maybe so, but at least I had Indira, and Joelle, and Christine that I could share it with. And maybe one of these days I could share it with Manuel too.

She jumped up and passed me her last cookie as the bell rang. "Wait for me at the bus after school," she said. "I'm going to help you solve that mystery or my name isn't Crystal Coral."

I said, "What are you talking about?" with a mouth full of cookie, just as she burst out laughing. "Oh, and for the record, I forgot to tell you. You're Luna LeFleur. Later!" Then she melted into the crowd pushing through the cafeteria doors into the noisy, teeming hallway.

I told Christine about the mystery of the locked suitcases as we walked from the bus stop to my house. "That's super weird and creepy," she said. "What do you think she's hiding?"

That's exactly what I'd been trying to figure out. "I'm not sure," I said. "The only thing I know for sure is she's acting really weird. She even stayed up and watched tv with me last night."

Christine didn't say anything then and I realized that she probably sat around and did all sorts of things like that with her mom. They probably even did each other's hair and gave each other pedicures. I swallowed hard as we walked up the long driveway to my house in silence.

I pushed the code on the garage door so we could go in the back door to the kitchen. "Wow!" she whispered as we entered the house. "I always forget how big and shiny your house is! You could fit a hundred people in here."

Maybe, I thought, but there's hardly ever been more than just the three of us in here. I set a bunch of snacks on the counter while I told her about the guy in the wheelchair from the newspaper and Joelle's discovery of her wheelchair guy at the park.

"I think we should tell Indira about this," Christine said, mixing granola into a big bowl of frozen yogurt. "Didn't she track you down before when you disappeared? Doesn't she love mysteries?"

"Ok," I agreed. "You're right. I just wanted to try figuring some of it out on my own." I explained about the boy in the yearbook and all the photographs hidden under my bed. "I think it's all connected somehow."

"This is just like Dateline!" Christine replied. "Let's get those suitcases open and see what's in there!" She kept talking more excitedly as she rinsed out her bowl and opened the dishwasher. "Oh, and I'll video you opening them and we can send it to Indira. Giving myself goosebumps just picturing it!"

She turned back around just in time to see me, standing next to the open kitchen drawer with my mouth in a big wide O and my eyes bulging, my arms covered in goosebumps too.

"What's up, Elinor? You look like you've seen a ghost."

"The keys," I croaked. "They're gone!"

TWENTY-SEVEN

Luna

When I recovered from the shock, I told Christine about Janna Faz opening her sister's diary with a paperclip. "We shall not be deterred from our mission!" I said as I rummaged through the drawer for a paper clip to use as a suitcase key. I found one clipping a bunch of receipts together and twisted it open. "Let's go!" I said hoisting it in the air in triumph. "Grab your phone, Christine, and prepare to document the evidence."

Seconds later we were at the door to the locked shed. I used the birthday code and it opened on the first try, the door swinging open with a whoosh of musty air. We stepped inside. I thought at first it must be a trick of the light, but soon enough realized the mystery had just deepened. The suitcases were no longer there. The corner of the shed where I'd seen them yesterday was empty.

I turned to Christine and said, "You can put your phone away. Somebody stole all our clues."

"Somebody doesn't want you to discover their secret," Christine replied. "Somebody is running scared."

I guess she didn't know that I was the one who was scared. What was in those suitcases and what didn't my mother want anyone to find out?

As we were dejectedly heading back into the house, our gardener's truck pulled up the drive to the side gate. "It's Martin," I told Christine. "Maybe he knows what happened."

It turns out he did. Sort of. "Miss Malcolm told me to keep the shed door locked in case of burglars. She told me Mr. Malcolm had invested in some expensive new tools and he didn't want them to go missing." He lifted a big white flowery plant from the bed of his truck as he spoke. "I don't question it, but I don't see any new tools either, you know. I just say, ok."

"Did you ever see anything weird in there? Like a suitcase or something?'

"In the shed? No, nothing weird. Just the usual stuff. Now if you'll excuse me Miss Elinor and friend, I've got to get this planted for your mamacita."

Christine turned back as he walked away. "Excuse me," she called to Martin. "I've never seen a plant like that before. What's it called?"

"This beauty here? Why this is what you call in English a moonflower. A flor de Luna."

Christine grabbed my arm as Martin entered the garden. "We've got to call Indira now!" she said. "She's the one who suggested Liza Wren change your name to Luna LaFleur in the book." She squeezed my arm tighter. "Moonflower!"

Indira didn't think it was weird at all. "It's just what I always tell you," she explained. "You've just got to stay open. That universe of ours lives inside us too – it's not just the part you can see. There are a million little miracles happening every day if you just pay attention. Everything is connected. Everything."

She explained how Liza Wren said she had to fictionalize our names since she was just basing her new novel on us – not writing a non-fiction book. So, she changed Christine Corrales to Crystal Coral *(a sparkly gem!)* and Indira to Athena because she's so wise and beautiful and she fights for her friends. Indira told me that she knew I'd want to be Daisy but that was just too ordinary for someone magical like me. That's the word she used – magical. She said I pulled people together like the moon pulls the tides. "You have powerful karma, Elinor who we adore. You *are* a moon flower, most definitely. Hence, you shall be called Luna LaFleur forevermore.

And as for that suitcase mystery, let's lay out all the clues you have so far and get to work. No way we can't figure it out if we put our minds to it. When is your friend from Oklahoma meeting with the wheelchair guy again? I'd bet the farm he holds the missing key."

Twenty-eight

Rescued

By the time we laid out all the clues, including the 1996 yearbook with the message from a boy named Curtis who signed it *love,* the pictures in the box in my mom's childhood closet with that same handsome boy holding her close, the newspaper clippings and folders stuffed with pages in the mysterious disappearing suitcases, the muddy tracks up the back stairs into my mom's office, and the padlocked shed, my head was spinning.

"I wonder why your grandma stopped visiting," Christine said. "I mean if your mom was so upset when she died, I wonder what they were fighting over."

"A-ha!" Indira shouted. "That's it! Add that to the list of clues. You're on to something, Sherlock!"

And before I had time to process Christine's question, which stunned me, I admit, she said her mom was on her way to pick her up and we'd have to continue the conversation later.

"No problem-o," Indira said. "Elinor and I can work on it tomorrow after we work on our poetry dance. In fact, our dance energy will help open up our heartspace for enlightenment. Once we get lost in the breath of movement, the puzzle pieces will pick up the vibration and just click together like magic. I can feel it."

We hung up before I told her there was no way I could get to The Healing HeARTs tomorrow without Christine.

I was awakened at 5:00 am by the buzzing of my phone. Joelle. She always forgets how early it is here.

Today's the day! she texted. Wheelchair basketball.

As if I could forget. Maybe now one major part of the mystery would finally be solved.

I rolled over and tried to fall back to sleep, but I just kept picturing my mom in her muddy slippers crouched next to that newspaper on her office floor, that mystery guy in the wheelchair staring up at me next to an old lady who could be my Grandma Ruth.

My phone buzzed again. OOWS!

OOWS?

It was Indira. She must have rolled over in her sleep and texted by mistake.

A few minutes later, CM 2 #rescu-u. ETA 7:30 AM 4 EM.

Was she sleep-texting? A confusing exchange followed where I figured out that *OOWS* was not a mistake – it simply meant *on our way shortly* in Indira speak. And CM was Carpool Mom, and ETA means exactly what everyone knows it means. EM, of course, is me, Elinor Malcolm. A puzzling message from Indira Makepeace, AKA Tiffany Woo, that I finally deciphered. That girl was the master of the cryptic clue!

She and her mom were driving all the way from the city to my house to take me to The Healing HeARTs today since Christine had band practice for her solo. When Christine called Indira last night, unbeknownst to me, and told her I couldn't make it to the city because I didn't have a ride, Indira said that was unacceptable, so she and her mom were setting out early, armed with coffee shakes and organic donuts to rescue me from suburban captivity and deliver me to my zenspace. At least that's what I concluded.

It felt like the universe was leading me somewhere that I wasn't sure I was ready for, but I never can say no to Indira. Or her mom, for that matter. So, I took a quick shower, threw on my yoga clothes, grabbed my mat and my notebook full of poems, and headed downstairs.

The sun was just getting up, and my mom would probably be asleep for another hour or so. I dashed off a quick note telling her not to worry – I had a ride to The Healing HeARTs and I'd be home in time for dinner. I added a *have a nice day* and a smiley-faced heart, then left the note next to the coffee pot where she'd be sure to find it, long after I'd gone. Then I went outside and crept down the driveway to wait on the stone wall for Indira and her mom. I felt like a character in my own story, dutifully following the author's plotline.

At 7:30 on the dot, a dusty minivan came slowly rolling up the street. The side door slid open, loud music came pouring out, and I hopped inside. Indira reached around from the front seat, passed me a shake and said, "Bonjour, Miss LaFleur." As the minivan pulled away from my house, Indira handed me a bag holding a still warm donut; her mom winked at me in the rear-view mirror and sang, "A body in motion stays in motion. That's a natural fact! We three ladies are definitely on the move! Getting our groove in an all-star act! Getting ready for a booty-shaking, memory-making day of sunshine, funshine and love."

The whole ride to the city was like that, filled with singing and wordplay between Indira and her mom, with me just sitting in the back smiling and singing along quietly, happy and grateful to be a passenger in their magical orbit.

TWENTY-NINE

Courage

This was one of the best mornings of my life.

First, that car ride. Then Indira leafing through my notebook to lift danceable lines for our performance.

Sunlight was streaming through the skylight, bathing the whole lobby in gold as we sat together in the corner. Everything just felt so warm and natural, like this is where I'm supposed to be. This is what I'm meant to be doing at this moment in my life.

"We're making a poem collage, a barrage of feelings, a true heart massage built with soul- searching cour*age* by the queen of the spoken word," Indira said, pronouncing it *cour – aj* with a French accent. "It comes, of course, chère, from *coeur*, the French word for heart." She patted my arm and then pulled a clump of rubber-banded markers from her bag.

"Remember," she said as she began jotting lines on separate pieces of lined cardstock paper that looked like those sentence strips from first grade, "you are a celestial body. We'd be nothing without your brilliant words to move us."

I admit, I felt a little bit like I was floating, watching her write out my words in blue, and purple, and orange ink. *"My grandmother left this world drenched in sky tears,"* and *"We are all connected to each other, across the days, across the years,"* and *"Your words, born in blood and anger, cut me to the quick"* and *"A dusty photograph is a faded dream to make you homesick for what you never knew."*

Once she had a whole stack on the table she said, "Now we wait for the magic."

She stood up, waved her hands across the pieces of the poetry puzzle, said "Namaste," and headed into the hallway. I jumped up and followed her into one of the small rehearsal spaces. "So," she said, "Let me show you the movement Christine and I have worked out so far."

We spread our yoga mats on the floor and she taught me the poses as she hummed a familiar melody. I told her about Christine playing the flute as part of our performance and she said, "Ah, that will add just the right measure of mellow to our Longfellow."

After what seemed like no time at all, the door opened and Indira's mom poked her head inside.

"Looking good, ladies. Time to finish up though. My Tai Chi class has this room booked next." We wiped down our mats and rolled them up while Mrs. Finkle-Woo stood there smiling at the two of us. She has the warmest smile, just like Indira. "And Liza Wren is waiting for you in the lobby."

My heart did a flip-flop. I hadn't exactly forgotten that I was going to meet her today, but in all the excitement of the morning, that idea got pushed to the back of my mind. I was definitely sweating then, and it wasn't from exercise. "You two will definitely hit it off," Indira said as we headed to the lobby. "She's a Cancer too."

There at our corner table covered with sentence strips filled with my poetry, sat the most beautiful woman I'd ever seen. Time seemed to stop as I stood there, rooted to one spot, unable to move. She had long red hair that fell in waves, brushing across the table top as she sorted the sentence strips in what felt like a slow motion movie scene.

"Liza!" Indira's voice boomed in my ear, startling me into motion. She thrust out her hand. "So good to see you again."

Liza Wren stood up. "And you must be…" she clasped both hands to her heart. "You must be my Luna."

Indira explained to her how she'd lifted lines of my poems to make a collage poem that we could dance to and how Christine was going to layer in some beautiful flute music and how we were planning to film it and upload it and how I was the one who made it all happen. "This girl here is the main character in our clever endeavors." Then she said she had to check people in and it would be the perfect time for the two of us to get to know one another.

I had never talked to a best-selling author before but she was just like a regular person. She told me how she got started as a writer in middle school by working on the yearbook and starting a school newspaper with her twin brother. She explained the process of writing novels in verse and how she starts every morning reading poetry and writing in her journal. And then she told me about how inspiration happens and how incredibly inspiring my story was.

"It's not really a story, though," I said. "It's just my life."

"Ah, but it's an extraordinary life, Elinor. You must know that. Your story is inspiring, to say the least. You follow your heart and everyone wants to follow along with you."

And just like that, the best morning of my life came to a screeching halt. There, standing in the doorway, looking very much out of place was the last person I expected to see at The Healing HeARTs.

My mother.

THIRTY

The Taming of the Shrew

hank goodness for Indira's mother, the magical Mrs. Shoshana Finkle-Woo. She came rushing into the lobby to see what all the commotion was, and she immediately disarmed my irate mother. "You must be Elinor's mum – she's your spitting image!" My mother stood there puffed up like a grizzly, stomping her foot, all red-faced and sweaty, her finger pointed accusingly at me sitting in the far corner with Liza Wren.

Mrs. Finkle-Woo continued, "It's so wonderful to finally meet you. We just adore this wonderchild of yours!" She grabbed my mother's outstretched hand. "Come, have a seat. You look like you could use some refreshment."

My mother sputtered, but then dropped into a chair at the nearest table. It was like she was under a spell, her mood suddenly tamed. "I was so worried! I woke up and she was gone," she whispered in a still quaking voice.

Mrs. Finkle-Woo slipped into the chair next to her and patted her hand while Indira dropped off a cup of steaming jasmine tea and a plate of chocolate chip zucchini bread. The speakers crackled — the awkward silence replaced by that soothing spa music that Indira uses in her yoga classes. Liza Wren squeezed my arm but I kept my eyes focused straight ahead, afraid to meet her eyes, embarrassed by what she must think of me now.

I strained to hear what they were saying to each other – there were lots more hand pats and head nods, but the piped in music blocked the sound. Finally, Indira's mom turned and looked at me, calling across the lobby filling with people stopping for brunch. "Elinor Malcolm, is it true you left the house without asking permission or telling your mom who was bringing you here today?"

"Well, I…"

"No excuses – just the truth. Yes or no?"

I could feel my face growing red, all eyes in the room now focused on me.

"I'm sorry. I didn't. I just wanted. Christine couldn't." I was not making any sense.

She stood then and rested her hand on my mom's shoulder. "Take a cleansing breath, dear. I believe you owe this wonderful woman who raised you your deepest, most sincere apology." And then, Indira's mom winked at me, a quick wink, a secret signal that no one else saw, but I suddenly understood.

"I'm sorry, Mom."

"And?" Indira's mom flicked her head toward my silent mom sitting there beside me, and I heard Indira's voice in my head. *You know what to do.*

I walked over, and put my arms around my mom's neck and kissed the top of her head. "I'm really, truly sorry, Mom. I didn't mean to worry you. I'm sorry."

I looked up just in time to catch Liza Wren madly scribbling away in her little notebook.

THIRTY-ONE

Heat of the Moment

By the time we left The Healing HeARTs later that day, several miracles had occurred. My mom agreed to come back next week to try a yoga class after Indira's mom told her how learning to breathe *with* your body is the number one trick of successful attorneys and celebrities. "I can't guarantee you'll win every case, but you'll definitely up your chances of making the cover of the National Law Journal!" was the statement that sealed the deal.

Liza Wren had complimented and charmed my mother too — finally getting her to agree to sit for an interview. "I'm thinking of publishing a series of essays about successful women, and it sounds like you've carved out quite an impressive career," she told her. Blushing, my mom ran a hand through her blonde spikes as the writer followed up with "I'll pitch it to my editor this afternoon!" Another deal sealed.

And miracle of miracles, my mom told me that Indira seems like a lovely girl and she can't wait to see the performance that we're working on with our other friend Christine. In fact, she said it sounds like we just might be the perfect act to book for a small reception she was planning in our garden next month. "Just an intimate gathering to celebrate the future, and, well I can't think of anything more fitting," is how she put it.

So instead of riding home in stony silence, we talked and laughed like a regular mother-daughter duo. I kept hearing Indira's voice in my head saying, *There's no story without you. You are the glue.* And for once, it didn't feel like I'd turned everything into a sticky mess. My mom and I were finally bonding.

I wished I could ask her about what was in those suitcases and what she was hiding but I really didn't want to ruin things. Her secret was safe with her for a little while longer.

Joelle went to the park after school Monday afternoon, but her wheelchair guy wasn't there, and she can't go today after school because she has an orthodontist appointment. "Pray for me," she texted, "I may be getting these stupid braces off in time for school pictures."

I don't like to waste my prayers so I added, "and please let her find out who my wheelchair guy is soon. The suspense is killing me! Amen."

Manuel passed me a note during Spanish that said, *I heard you're a poet. Me too.*

Be still my heart.

I wonder if he knew I had a whole notebook in my backpack devoted to him.

I felt my face growing hot. Before I could stop myself, I quickly jotted *Write one for me?* below his message. I pushed the note back across the desk while Ms. Lopez was writing the homework on the board.

We were packing up our notebooks as the bell rang and he dropped a folded note into my open backpack. Ms. Lopez was looking right at us then. I couldn't risk her asking me to hand it over, so I quickly pulled the zipper closed and said, a little too loudly, "Oh thanks, I didn't see that I'd dropped that."

I'd have to wait till we were out of there to retrieve it and see what he wrote. I made a mad dash for the bathroom and locked the stall door.

Roses are red
Violets are not
Elinor Malcolm
I think U R hot!

Thirty-Two
Inspiration

I couldn't concentrate the rest of the day. By the time I got to yearbook after school, I was a total mess. I didn't know whether to give one of the poems I'd written about Manuel to him tomorrow or write him a whole new one about the stars aligning and poets' hearts entwining or something. I kept running all sorts of poetic phrases through my mind about those dark eyes, and that artist's heart, and that dimple that deepened whenever he smiled at me.

Christine wanted to know what was up, but I shrugged my shoulders and said, "Nothing. Why?"

"Well, you just seem so distracted. Are you worried about that science test tomorrow?"

McHenry, who doesn't seem to get boundaries, interrupted, wanting to know if I thought today was a good day to talk to Loveless about helping us start a school newspaper. Christine rolled her eyes. How could I tell him that was the furthest thing from my mind at the moment? He's as impulsive and sincere as that puppy dog logo on his shirt.

Ms. Loveless flicked the lights and told us she had an announcement. "Listen up all you ace reporters and rock-star editors. My partner in crime, Elinor slash Editor, has been hard at work all week coming up with a theme for this year's book." She gave me a knowing look, then burst into one of her annoying snorty laughs. "Good times!"

Yikes. I had completely forgotten Why me?

"We'll announce the theme at the end of today's meeting. But for now, grab a piece of pizza, grab your partner, and get to work on your assignments. Chop, chop. Let's go!"

Theme. I pictured my mother's 1996 yearbook – nothing seemed memorable except for the things people wrote about her and that boy named Curtis who wanted to make the summer one to remember. I tried visualizing all the old yearbooks we'd looked at in here the first day where all we did was laugh at people's clothes and hair. Not cool.

What would be memorable? Everybody was counting on me. I set my backpack in the corner, and pulled out my poem from Manuel one more time.

Roses are red, Violets are not…

Where does inspiration come from? What did Liza Wren tell me?

Sometimes it's born of a deadline. Like now!

Sometimes it comes from thinking about a special person. Like Manuel.

Sometimes it comes from your own heart's desire. Like poetry.

Elinor Malcolm. I think U R hot

"I've got it!" I told Ms. Loveless as I joined her behind the library counter where she was typing her grades into the library computer.

She lifted a finger to signal *just a minute,* then said, "Ta-da. Done!" and closed the gradeloop app. She swiveled around on the librarian's stool to look at me standing there wearing a triumphant smile. "So, what have you got?"

"Ok," I ventured. "This might be a little bit much, but what if," I swept the hair out of my eyes, took a deep breath, and continued, "what if we called it the Valley Poetry Collection?"

"I'm listening," she said, straightening her stack of papers before stuffing them into the briefcase on the counter beside her. "I'm all ears."

"Well, what if we spelled it "Poetree" and the cover was a tree and the branches were made up of the names of every student at Valley Middle School?"

"Go on." She hopped off the stool and shoved her feet into those incredibly ugly shoes with the smashed down heels.

"And then we could have sections like *Poetry in Motion* for sports, and *Love Poems* for pictures of couples doing fun things like bowling and stuff, and, well that's all I've got so far, but what do you think?"

"What do I think Miss Malcolm? I'll tell you what I think. I think I definitely picked the right kid to be the Editor of the Valley Poetree Collection."

THIRTY-THREE

Teamwork

It was a little harder to convince the rest of the yearbook staff that doing something different would be a good thing until McHenry spoke. He can be very convincing for a little sixth grader. "The easy thing would be to do what's always been done. Just your typical ho-hum yearbook."

Brit, one of the usually clueless band girls, interrupted, "But what if everybody likes the same old-same old? What if they think ours is stupid?"

McHenry moved to the front of the room, his voice growing louder as he held up last year's yearbook. "I mean you've got to admit, this is pretty boring with a capital B! But we," he aimed his pointer finger at all of us in one big sweeping motion, "we have a chance to leave a lasting legacy. We can change the course of history."

"Yes!" Christine rose to her feet, shouting, "I get it now. Everybody wants to be famous. Everybody wants to see their name in lights, right?" She grabbed a dry erase marker off the counter and started a sketch on the whiteboard. "I think," she said, "this is what Elinor was picturing. Something like this!"

The energy in the room shifted as she stepped away from the board, *cools* and *wows* filling the charged air.

"And like poems have lots of rhyme and rhythm so like the band pages could be like *The Rhythm Section*," said Brit, jumping to her feet.

"The section with everybody's class picture in it could be called *Poetic Images!*" Sasha said before hi-fiving Brit.

"I have an idea," one of the eighth graders from last year added. "What if we made everyone's information under their picture into a haiku? I'm really good at that!"

I was sitting in the middle of it all, watching everyone get all excited about my idea. My idea! By the time the bell rang to signal it was time for all after-school clubs to end, we were a real team, focused on one goal – to make the coolest, most poetic yearbook that's ever been made.

Ms. Loveless stood by the door clapping her hands together like a little kid as we packed up our stuff.

I told Christine I'd text her later, and asked McHenry to save me a seat on the late bus. Once everybody was gone, I picked up the empty pizza boxes from the counter and dumped them in the trashcan while Ms. Loveless got the lights. "Thanks, kid," she said as we walked out together.

"Ok, partner," I said. "See you tomorrow!" Then I ran to catch the bus.

THIRTY-FOUR

Issues

By the end of the week, I had managed to write seven more poems about Manuel that I didn't give to him. I had exchanged a dozen text messages with Joelle who still hadn't heard from the wheelchair guy. I'd helped my mom learn how to do downward dog and warrior so she wouldn't embarrass herself in her first yoga class at the The Healing HeARTs on Saturday. I still couldn't believe she was going there with me and afterwards we'd be grabbing lunch with Christine and her mom and Indira and hers. The Three Prima Yogarinas and their cool moms taking the city by storm. Or at least being treated to a fancy lunch by my mom, the newest member of the bunch.

I hadn't worked up the nerve to ask her about her high school boyfriend and the mysterious suitcases that had been locked in the shed and if there was a connection. There were still too many missing puzzle pieces. I waited till we were in the car headed to dinner Friday night to broach the subject. "I'm so glad Dad will be home next week. I've really missed him, haven't you?" I began.

"I'll be happy he's back," she said, "but I try not to miss him too much when he's gone. I just put my energy in other places."

I turned up the air conditioning and turned down the music so I could concentrate. "Like where?"

"Oh, for goodness sake, Elinor. Like in my work, and paying the bills, and ordering the groceries, and taking care of you. You can't miss somebody so much when you're busy living your actual life."

Was that true? Didn't I miss him even when I was studying for science, or writing in my journal? Didn't I miss him even when I was watching tv or doing the dishes?

"You should try to compartmentalize a little more," she said. Could she read my mind? "It will save you a lot of heartache in life."

I tried again. "I forgot to tell him about my yearbook idea when we FaceTimed last night. Yearbooks are so cool, don't you think?"

She turned the car from First Street into the parking lot. "Yearbooks are completely overrated. They're like gossip magazines if you want to know the truth. Everybody crafts an image and then everybody says stuff like *stay as sweet as you are* when they really don't think you're sweet at all. When they'd rather stab you in the back."

I was staring at her with my mouth hanging open a little bit. She turned off the car and put her hand on the armrest. "Oh, sorry," she said, before reaching into the backseat for her purse. "I guess I still have a few unresolved issues!" She let out an uncomfortable laugh and opened the car door. "I'm sure your yearbook will be different though. It's got poems in it, right?"

"So, tell me all about poetry walk idea of yours," my mom said as the waiter put a basket of warm bread in front of us in the corner booth. "You want to display poems throughout the garden, am I getting it right?"

I could feel my phone vibrating in my pocket as I reached for the dipping sauce but I knew enough not to sneak a look. Phones during dinner were absolutely out of the question in my house even though my mom had no problem disregarding the rule when she was working on a big case. I tried to stay focused on the conversation at hand but I was wondering who kept texting me. Joelle?

Christine? Indira? It felt urgent and I was stuck here in the dark.

"Just one poem. But forget it. You probably won't like it." Bzzz. Bzzz.

"Now, why wouldn't I like something you dreamed up? Honestly, Elinor, you have to have more confidence in yourself."

"Ok, well it's actually really cool. Christine said she'd help me design it." Bzzz. Bzzz. "She's a really good artist."

"What is that awful buzzing sound, Elinor? Your phone?"

"Hmm, maybe, I guess so." I stared at the menu. "I didn't notice. Can I order a salad?" Bzzz. Bzzz.

"For goodness sake, please turn that all the way off so we can enjoy our dinner."

I reached into my pocket, and pulled out my phone to turn it off. Before the screen went dark, I saw the text that was from Joelle. OMG. Call me!!!

THIRTY-FIVE

Signs

After dinner my mom wanted to go shopping in that fancy athletic store that sells yoga pants for about a million dollars a pair. "We've got to get outfitted for our big day tomorrow. You don't want to be embarrassed by your old mom wearing last year's number now, do you?"

"Nobody cares, Mom." She was not making this easy. "The Healing HeARTs isn't like that. You can just be yourself. Can't we just go home?"

"I do not understand you, Elinor. You're always craving time with me and then when I try to make it fun, you're an old stick in the mud," she said as we pulled into the mall. "You hardly said a word through dinner, you didn't want to order dessert, and now you don't want to hang out at the mall and do some serious damage in

LotusBlossom."

"I just have a lot of homework, and it's late." I was hyper aware of the turned off phone in my pocket and the weight of the unread message from Joelle.

"Oh, for crying out loud, it's eight o'clock on a Friday night, Elinor. So, I suggest you put a smile on your face and prepare to enjoy an evening on the town with your mother. Let's go!"

One of the things I'll never be able to understand is how you can be thinking about somebody and then there they are coming around the corner. Indira always says it's because our brains are so powerful. "You send out signals, like invisible waves," she once told me. "Think of it like this – you pick up the remote and point it at the tv, and the tv goes on. Well, your brain is like the remote – if your spirit is in sync with the universe, you point your thoughts at somebody and voila!"

I was thinking about that because as I was looking through the racks and stacks in LotusBlossom, I was imaging what Manuel might say if he saw me wearing a top like this hot pink one, or these yoga capris. And then I started thinking about that poem he wrote for me that said *Elinor Malcolm, I think U R hot*, and then I started picturing the first time he said, *Hey, New Girl* and then I was picturing that dimpled smile of his and…

"I said, do you want to try those on? Can I start a room for you?" A tall blonde girl was taking the pile of clothes out of my arms.

"Oh, sorry," I said, "I didn't hear you. I was just…"

"No worries," she said. "Happens all the time. We call it the trance. Picturing how your life will change once you're wearing LotusBlossom."

I started following her to the dressing room when I got that weird goose-bumpy feeling that I get sometimes when I'm about to freak out. I stopped dead in my tracks. Standing at the checkout counter with a tall, beautiful dark-haired girl, there he was, the boy of my dreams.

Manuel didn't see me as he put his arm around her and left the store.

I couldn't sleep. When we finally got home and I called Joelle, she had that *unavailable* message on her phone that her mother makes her put on after 11:00 pm and it was way later than that in Oklahoma. I couldn't even leave a message. Then I texted Christine to tell her that I saw Manuel with another girl at the mall and she texted back, What did I tell you? Trouble! I didn't respond.

My mother's words came back to haunt me. *Beware of those pretty boys. They'll break your heart.*

I climbed out of bed, put on some soft music, and tried to do some stretches in the dark to get into my calm space. Everything was swirling around in my head – all these questions with no answers. A quiet knock brought me back to the present. The door opened slightly and my mom poked her head in. "Ah, couldn't sleep?" she whispered. I nodded. "Me neither. I guess I'm more excited about tomorrow than I knew," she said as she lowered herself next to me on my mat.

We sat there in silence for a long time.

"This is nice," she said. "I can see why you're so into this."

I almost asked her then. I knew she had the key to all my unanswered questions, but I didn't want to spoil the mood.

"Yeah," I said. "Sorry about tonight."

She put her arm around me and pulled me close. "All's well that ends well," she said. "Now let's say we both get some sleep. Big day tomorrow."

THIRTY-SIX

Luck Be A Lady

When I got through to Joelle first thing this morning, her *OMG* news was on the disappointing side. She didn't have any real news yet, but she thought she might have a lead. A pretty weak one if you ask me. The wheelchair guy finally showed up at the park and apologized for not coming back sooner. He got sort of injured in his basketball game and had to rest up for a little while but he was better now. He never got around to asking if anybody there knew an old lady named Mrs. Frisbie, but he told her there's an interesting picture of some old lady at the place where they play their games. "She looks important," he said. "Maybe it's who you're looking for."

"That's hardly news," I told her. "Do you know how many old ladies live in Tulsa?"

"I know, I know," she said. "But I got goosebumps when he said it, so it just felt like a lead worth following. Anyway, I'm gonna check it out today. Wish me luck!"

Maybe if I focused my thoughts on Grandma Ruth instead of on Manuel and that pretty girl he was with at the mall I could change the course of history. Or at least maybe I wouldn't feel so crummy.

I put on the bright pink top I'd bought the night before with Manuel in mind, and headed downstairs. "Fake it till you make it, fake it till you make it," was a song playing over and over in my head.

There was music coming from the kitchen along with something that smelled really delicious and homemade. I have never seen my mom like this. She was singing along to the music coming from her phone. She was wearing one of her new yoga outfits and drinking some greenish shake while she sliced into a loaf cooling on the counter. "Thought we'd better have a hearty breakfast before our big day." She passed me a huge slice on a plate. "It's blueberry drizzle. And there's more shake in the blender. *Bon Appétit!*"

"How?" I stammered. "Why? I mean you must have been up for hours already!"

She handed me a fork and took a sip of her shake. "Talked to Dad early, early, and then thought since I'm already awake, I might as well make myself useful. I know how you love coffee cake."

I think the last time she baked anything for me was my ninth birthday. That was also the last time my Grandma Ruth stepped foot in our house.

On our way to The Healing HeARTs she asked me all about Christine and Indira and asked me to tell her again how we came to be the Prima Yogarinas. She asked me to fill in the details about my plans for making a poetry walk in the garden and said she thought it would be lovely to include the moms in the little garden party she was planning next month. I recited the lines of the garden poem for her and she said, "My word, Elinor. You really are a poet. My word!"

At the studio she took three classes in a row. "Marsha, girl, you are a natural!" Indira's mom said as we were heading to lunch. "I see where Elinor gets it." And at the restaurant my mom announced, "The tea leaf salad here is to die for, but order anything you like. It's on me." Mrs. Corrales and Mrs. Finkle-Woo tried to protest, but my mom raised her hand and said, "No, no. I won't hear of it. You are all so special to my daughter and so you're special to me too." Then she tapped on her water class with her knife and said, "A toast! To friendship!"

This was not the Marsha Malcolm that I was used to seeing. She was smiling and laughing and she looked like the girl in the photographs stashed under my bed. She looked like the girl in the yearbook with a boyfriend named Curtis. I didn't know what had changed, but I did not want to chance ruining it all. I decided then and there to forget about the mysterious suitcases and the yellowed newspapers. I didn't need to go digging into the past. I wanted to stay right here in this present with this mother and these friends.

We stayed there talking and swapping stories until we were the only people left in the restaurant and the waiter asked for the third time, "Will there be anything else?"

My mom said, "Actually, yes, if you don't mind. Can you take our photo? I think we need to memorialize this occasion."

Indira raised her hand like we were in school. "Actually, factually," she said, standing and handing him her phone. "Make it post-able. We're about to hit it big!"

He moved back a few steps and held the phone at eye level. "Smile ladies!"

"Wait, wait!" Indira said, "We need to offer our gratitude to the unstoppable force that brought us here today. On the count of three, say it loud and proud with me.

To love!

To amor!

To our fierce and feisty, Elinor!"

The waiter took a few more photos, then passed Indira's phone back to her. "Good day then, ladies. Thank you for dining with us," he said, giving a slight bow in our direction. "And good luck with whatever."

"We," I said, "don't need luck. We've got each other."

It turns out a little more luck might have been helpful. Or actually, maybe a little less.

THIRTY-SEVEN

Exhibit A

U sitting down?

The text was from Joelle.

I shifted on the bench out in the garden where I'd been listening to the birds and picturing my poetry walk and dreaming about a little garden party with my friends and their moms.

When I called her cell, she answered excitedly, "It's your lucky day!" Joelle said she found the place where the wheelchair athletes play their basketball games and it's right next to the park.

"We passed it when we went there this summer when you were here," she said, "but you probably didn't notice it." She told me that it's just an old, ugly cinderblock building that used to be a jail. Inside it's all colorful and modern though, with a cool reception area and some glassed-in offices and a small gym. That's where the guys play, but it was pretty empty when she got there except for a custodian who was waxing the gym floor. Now it's called the Path2Peace Center.

"Is that why I'm sitting down?" I asked. "To hear about some old building by the park?"

"Sorry," Joelle said. "No, here's the thing. I looked all around but I didn't see anybody or anything that would help solve your mystery. But then when I was leaving, it was right there, staring down at me." She paused dramatically. "Over the door," she added conspiratorially.

"What?" I was sweating then. I felt my happy Saturday afternoon melting away.

"A giant copper plaque over the entrance that said, *Path2Peace made possible due to our generous benefactor.* And Elinor, maybe I should just show you."

There on my screen, the newspaper photograph that had been haunting me for weeks appeared, except now it was in the form of a huge framed photograph hanging on a wall next to a giant copper plaque in a transformed jail in Tulsa, Oklahoma.

No matter how much I try to be content living in the moment, the past just keeps pulling me back.

I couldn't stop thinking about how Indira would say *You know what to do,* but this time I really didn't. I wanted things to stay perfect, just the way they were earlier today. I didn't want to solve the mystery anymore. I didn't want to know who he was and what he had to do with my Grandma Ruth, and what that had to do with my mom, but I also didn't want to not know. I wished I'd never opened that box in my mom's childhood closet. I wished I'd never opened those suitcases. I wished I'd never unlocked the shed. I wished I'd never set this whole unraveling of the past in motion.

The rest of the weekend I fought the urge to mention my discovery to my mom and wreck our new bond. I fought the urge to google Path2Peace and dive deeper into the abyss. I concentrated on the here and now. I practiced yoga poses in the den with my mom. I FaceTimed with my dad who'll be home in just a few days. I worked on a design for the poetry walk with Christine. I worked on more poems for our yogarina performance, and I sketched out more ideas for the yearbook. I stayed busy and concentrated on the present and it actually worked.

In school on Monday, I avoided all the places Manuel usually hangs out, and I made sure not to make eye contact when he came into Spanish class. I stared straight ahead when he tried to pass me a note and got caught by Ms. Lopez who said, "I'll take that, Mr. Garcia. Thank you." Instead of handing it over though, he did something I wouldn't have believed if I didn't see it with my own eyes. He popped the whole note into his mouth and began chewing.

Ms. Lopez lost control of the class for a minute while she stood there, mouth agape, but she quickly regained composure and quieted everyone by announcing, "You, sir, can head to the office. They'll be expecting you!"

Manuel stood up slowly and sauntered across the room while everyone stared and Ms. Lopez called down to the office to let them know he was on his way. After he left, everyone turned their attention to me, but Ms. Lopez didn't seem to notice. "Now then, where were we?" she asked before continuing the vocabulary drill while my mind drifted back to the mall. Instead of following along, I ignored my classmates' stares. I slid my journal of poems dedicated to Manuel into my open textbook, and started another one.

> *Be careful what you do in the dark*
> *When you think no one is watching*
> *Be careful you don't break a heart*
> *When you're trying to play it so cool*

I couldn't help wondering what that chewed up note to me said. I was still wondering when the bell rang.

THIRTY-EIGHT

From the Heart

When I got home from school, my mom's car was parked in the garage. She called to me from her office as I came through the back door. "Elinor, I'm so glad you're home. Come here. You'll never believe it!"

It turns out she'd spent the better part of the day with Liza Wren. "It was more like a therapy session," she said. "She's going to use my photo on the cover of *Evolution*, her new book about successful women. Can you believe it?"

"Evolution? Like Darwin?"

"No," she laughed. "It's *Evolution: Ten Remarkable Stories of Growth and Resilience.* And I get the cover." My mom was sitting at her desk in front of her laptop, and she was glowing with pride and happiness. She told me how Liza had her she trace her history from small town nobody to successful prosecutor and it was like a heavy weight had been lifted as she recounted her complicated journey from then to now. "Telling your story is cathartic," she said. "All this guilt and shame I'd kept buried, all finally made sense when it played out in my story arc."

I sat down at that point. "What were you ashamed of?" I asked. I sort of didn't want to know. My brain kept saying, *don't open that box, don't unlock that door*, but I couldn't tame my curiosity. "You're so successful, why would you be guilty about that?" The picture Joelle sent me from Path2Peace flashed before my eyes.

"Oh, Elinor," she said, as she closed the laptop, "not about being successful, but about all the wreckage strewn along the way." She stood up and walked over to where I was sitting on the sofa and plopped down next to me. "But here's the thing, Elinor." She put her arm around me and pulled me in close. She smelled like roses. "Liza made me realize all my success in life is not about money, or this house, or the international travel, or the law. You're my big success. You and Dad. You're my everything."

I closed my eyes and snuggled into her, settling into the moment, wishing it could last.

I was still floating when I got to the bus stop in the morning. My dad would be getting home late tonight. He said tomorrow we could have our Japanese movie marathon, even though it was a school night. "One groggy morning will not spoil your GPA," he said from the airport lounge in Osaka. "And don't forget to order the sushi. I'm bringing you wagashi. Remember the first time we shared it?"

I missed him so much, and now he'd be home. I couldn't believe how much had happened in the short time he'd been away. I wonder if he'd notice the change in my mom. The change in me?

I daydreamed all the way to school and thought I must still be dreaming when I stepped off the bus. There was Manuel, standing right there on the sidewalk, hands in his pockets, mega-watt smile, waiting for me.

"Hey, Chica. This one hasn't been chewed," he said, holding out a folded note as I walked toward the entrance.

I kept walking, and he fell in right beside me. "From the heart. El corazón."

"I thought you were always late to school," I said as I got to my locker.

"My sister got up early to drive me. So I could see you. So I could give this to you."

"Too bad," I said as I began turning the lock. I really wanted to see what he wrote, but I couldn't let him know that. He already had a girlfriend, obviously.

"Okay," he said. "I can take a hint. Just thought you were different." He walked away as the first bell rang, then turned back around quickly as the hallway filled with noise. And then he was gone.

When I got to homeroom, Ms. Loveless said, "Some boy just asked me to give this to you. He said you dropped it." Then she dropped a very wrinkled note on my desk with a wink. "And, you're welcome."

I quickly shoved it into my pocket and pretended to read my book until the bell rang and I could escape her curious stare.

THIRTY-NINE

Exhibit B

At home I reread the poem from Manuel a dozen times.

Like the pull of the moon on the ocean tides
I'm swept into your eyes so deep,
your heart so open, your smile so wide
I didn't want to move, but now I'm glad
You took away the pain inside
Ever since my papa died

How phony could one boy be? He was a pretty good poet though, that's for sure.

Beware of the pretty boys. They'll break your heart.

I grabbed my laptop out of my backpack and tried to start my homework, but it was so hard to concentrate. I needed to finish up my lab report today so I could watch that movie with my dad tomorrow. As I was typing, a message came across the top of my screen alerting me to a new email message. From Joelle. I never use email and neither does she. I ignored it.

A few minutes later, a text. Just sent you an email. Urgent.

I really wish I hadn't opened it. But I did, and now there was nothing I could do to erase what I saw. There was no turning back.

"Duh! Why didn't we do this before?" Joelle wrote. "I did a little google search and *ay carumba!* We hit the jackpot here. Call me if you want to talk."

There were four attachments to her email, one worse than the other.

The first one was a fairly recent article about the founding of the Path2Peace and the anonymous donor who purchased the building that now houses the organization. It said in part, "Path2Peace was begun by a victims' rights group to teach non-violence in the schools and raise money for educational programs. They promote the need for communities to rebuild hope and trust and to show that the human spirit is made to triumph over tragedy."

Another article was an interview with Grandma Ruth, who said she first became aware of the organization when she read an article about the 20th anniversary of a brutal incident that happened at ConcertCity when a young man was nearly beaten to death for making a pass at a girl. "That article just dredged up all sorts of feelings in me," she's quoted as saying. "The good lord spoke to my heart, and I just knew I had to do something."

Next was a very brief article about high school sweethearts and class officers Marsha Frisbie and Curtis Crowe both being accepted at Oklahoma State where they hoped to major in social work in the fall of 1996.

And finally, there was an article with that picture that I'd already seen too many times – a guy in a wheelchair and Grandma Ruth standing behind him with her hand on his shoulder. The article detailed how happy she was to help get him back on his feet after learning he'd been in a nursing home for the past two decades with a brain and spinal cord injury.

I felt like my heart was breaking, and I wasn't even sure for who. For my Grandma Ruth? My mom? Some guy I didn't know? Myself?

This is not the kind of information that's easy to take in. I felt like I was going to be sick.

I closed my laptop and pulled the covers up over my head. Maybe this was all a bad dream. If I fell asleep, maybe I could wake up later and there'd be no text from Joelle. No urgent email. No googled articles. No puzzle pieces that I'd have to sort and process. What was I supposed to do with this unsettling information now that I had it?

FORTY

Treachery

It's so comforting sitting here in the dark, watching this movie with my dad tonight while he's telling me all about his trip. We're kind of watching and talking at the same time. The movie has subtitles so I kind of miss what's happening on the screen when he's talking, but I don't mind. I'm so glad he's home.

I haven't been able to look my mom in the eye since I read those articles Joelle found. I feel like I don't even really know her. My dad asked her to watch the movie with us tonight but she said she had some important research to do and we should just enjoy getting reconnected.

"Elinor and I have had lots of special times together while you've been away," she said. I couldn't help wondering what it was she was researching, and wishing I had not been so interested in uncovering her packed away secrets which now felt like my burden to bear. Alone. Wasn't it my mom who always told me, be careful what you wish for?

As the credits were rolling, my dad said, "Ok, Elliebear, it's late, you better just head up to bed. I'll take care of the clean-up."

I snuggled in closer. "Dad?" I whispered, afraid I'd lose my nerve. "Can I ask you something?"

"You, my dear, can ask me anything. Unless it's if you can stay up later." He kissed the top of my head.

"I was wondering about why Mom came to college here, in California. Why didn't she go to like Oklahoma State College or something?"

He started to laugh. "Are you thinking about college already? Planning to up and go thousands of miles away like your mom?"

"No, just wondering." I had to squeeze my eyes shut tight so I wouldn't start crying.

"Well," he said, clicking off the TV, "you could probably ask her yourself, but if you want to know what I think, I'd say it was so she could find me, and have you, and live out her destiny. Here with us is where she's meant to be." He stood up then. "And upstairs in bed dreaming about algebra or cute boys is where you need to be, right now."

I tried to push the darkness out of my mind, but it kept pushing its way back in. I thought being in school would help, but it was making it worse.

First, in homeroom Ms. Loveless says, "You look like you got hit by a truck or something, partner. Boy trouble?" Next, period, I'm stung by the list of vocabulary words at the end of the chapter in my history book I'm supposed to be reading: *betrayal, perfidy, scandalous, treachery, combatant.* Mr. Hoy says, "Make sure you understand what the founders were trying to convey when they wrote these words. They're very specific."

Then in science, my lab partner hands me the directions for our simple machines experiment and the bolded words on the page jump out at me and lodge there in my brain: *inquiry, wedge, screw, force, result.* It's like everything is connected to the trauma in my life. I can't do this, I think.

I raise my hand and ask if I can go to the nurse.

Lying on the cot in the darkened space there, I keep repeating my mother's trick. *Compartmentalize. Compartmentalize. Compartmentalize.*

I try picturing the performance Indira and

Christine and I are almost finished polishing, but in my mind's eye, I keep messing up my part. I forget the words. I don't remember the moves. My feet feel like they're stuck in quicksand and I'm moving in slow motion while Christine and Indira signal for me to stop and take it from the top. That's when I hear Indira's familiar voice. It sounds like she's right here next to me. *You know what to do*, she says. *You've got this.*

When the nurse comes in to take my temperature, I tell her I'm feeling better, and I do. I know what to do.

First, I get to Spanish early and give the poem I wrote to Manuel. He studies it for a long time, and then says, "I don't get it. What did I do in the dark?"

"You're a poet," I say. "It's a metaphor. Figure it out." I'm remembering Indira's words from the other day, *our fierce and feisty, Elinor* but I'm actually shaking a little bit when I say it.

"That's not helpful," he says as the bell rings.

"You're a big phony-baloney," I say quickly as Ms. Lopez begins taking roll.

He doesn't answer, just turns away and opens his Spanish book. He doesn't look at me once all period, and that's just fine with me.

When I get home, I read through my mother's yearbook one more time and check to make sure. Yup, that handsome boy who wrote *Let's make it a summer to remember, love Curtis* is the same guy who's in that photograph with Grandma Ruth. Except that he's twenty years older. And no longer smiling. Or wearing a tuxedo. Or able to stand up.

I gather all the old photographs and stack them neatly on top of the yearbook, and I refold all the '90's t-shirts that I've been wearing. I change into the one that says *Strong Enough*, and then I print out the articles that Joelle sent me. I know what I have to do.

I stay in my room until I hear my parents talking in the kitchen, and then I practice a few yoga moves. Warrior. Tree. Mountain. I take a few deep cleansing breaths, and then I head downstairs.

They are sitting at the kitchen table. They are leaning towards each other, their heads nearly touching. The kitchen feels so warm and inviting. For a minute I start to lose my nerve, but then I push ahead. They both look up in surprise as I deposit it all on the table – the t-shirts, the photographs, the yearbook, the articles.

"We need to talk," I say in my strongest voice. "It's urgent."

FORTY-ONE

Sound Sleep

hings are not always as simple as they seem. It's a lesson I keep learning over and over. I didn't know what to expect, but my mom and dad actually didn't get mad at me for taking all the things out of my mother's old closet in Tulsa. They didn't get mad at me for spying, and breaking into the shed, and trying to track down the whereabouts of the locked suitcases. They told me they were proud of me for being brave and initiating this conversation.

"Curiosity is actually a very good trait to have," my dad told me. "We want you to always stay curious about the world. Be an observer. Wonder. Question. Research." I breathed a sigh of relief. Like a giant, quivering sigh. My eyes were filled with tears that didn't fall. "But," he continued solemnly, "just make sure you don't jump to conclusions. Be a critical thinker. Check your resources. Ask for confirmation."

And then they took me step by step through my mom's journey from the summer of 1996 to today. They filled in all the details about Curtis Crowe who she almost married, but didn't. To the fight that changed everything. To a boyfriend in a nursing home who no longer knew who she was and to an unexpected change in plans that changed the trajectory of her life. Together, they told me about my mom's serendipitous decision to move to California, and their good luck at getting assigned to the same physics class at Berkeley. They talked about my mom's social work degree and her passionate interest in the law and her career focused on prosecuting victims of violent crime.

They answered all my questions and helped me understand how my Grandma Ruth made my mom feel ashamed when she started appearing in public and in newspaper articles with Curtis, dredging up the past. "If I had stayed," my mom said through her tears, "you wouldn't be here. That's what I couldn't make your grandma understand," she said. "I wanted her to just let the past stay in the past. But she couldn't."

"Your grandma was a very stubborn woman," my dad said. Then he winked and said, "sort of like you know who," he pointed at my mom, "and you know who." That gesture was to me. All three of us burst out laughing at that. He always knows how to lighten the mood.

We spent the rest of the evening huddled together on the couch, eating Chinese takeout and looking through all our old family albums. And I got to stay up late for the second night in a row. But this time, when I climbed into bed, I fell sound asleep.

FORTY-TWO

Tuesday Newsday

My dad drove me to school the next morning after they let me sleep in a little bit. He made me a Saturday breakfast of chocolate chip pancakes even though it was only Tuesday. My mom was on the phone with Liza Wren when we left, talking about an idea she had for writing a book of her own.

We pulled up to school behind a rusty pickup truck. "That is a heap and a half," my dad said. "I wonder who drives that old thing?" But I didn't have to wonder long, as the passenger door opened and Manuel Garcia hopped out. I wanted to wait till he was gone so I wouldn't have to talk to him, but my dad said, "Time's a-wastin,' Elliebear. You're already late enough as it is." He pushed the button to unlock my door. "See you tonight for a family Scrabble match?"

"Ok," I said. "And thanks again for being such a cool dad." I jumped out. "Have a splendiferous day!"

He beeped good bye and called out, "Fair warning, that is not a Scrabble word! So don't even think about trying it!" He waved as he pulled away from the curb, and I headed to the office.

And once again, Manuel and I were standing together at the counter, asking for a late pass. "Wait for me after school today," he whispered to me while the office lady was on the phone. "I need to talk to you."

After school was yearbook, so I didn't wait for him, I just bee-lined it to the library where everybody was still all excited about our *Poetree of Life at Valley Middle School* yearbook project. While I was showing Ms. Loveless my latest ideas for section headings, McHenry plopped down all excited. "Did Elinor tell you about our idea for starting a school newspaper? Could you help us get it started?"

Ms. Loveless looked like someone had just told her she looked like a million bucks or something. She got all puffed up and had this goofy smile that twitched a little bit, like she was trying not to show how flattered she was. I guess everybody needs to be needed.

McHenry enumerated all the reasons it was a good idea, but she said it wasn't possible because there was no budget for it, and she already could hardly keep up with her workload and all the extra duties teachers have to sign up for. "Let's get this yearbook of ours launched and make it the best darned yearbook this school has ever seen, and then we can talk about stretching our journalistic muscles next year. Okay?"

It looked sort of like the wind got knocked out of McHenry. His typically upbeat personality deflated and he shrunk even smaller in his seat.

"But, how about this?" she added. "What if I give you a little leeway and let you make a sort of newspaper inside the yearbook? You could be the editor of the Poetry Beat section and you could spotlight some interesting 8th graders like the Tie Brigade and the Environmental Club. And then next year, Mr. Plouffe, who knows?" Snort. "Who knows?"

And just like that he was jumping out of his seat and dancing across the room again. "Oh, yeah! Oh, yeah!" For a little sixth grader he sure doesn't care how goofy he looks in front of a bunch of seventh and eighth graders. I guess you've got to admire that confidence.

An hour later, we were all walking out of the meeting together—me, McHenry, Christine, the other band girls, the eighth graders, even Ms. Loveless. We felt like a real team. Our yearbook was going to rock and we all knew it.

As we came around the corner, I saw him standing there waiting. Manuel Garcia, with the amber-flecked eyes and the dimpled smile, and the poet's heart, and the won't-take-no for an answer personality was standing by the late bus waiting for me.

FORTY-THREE

Wonder. Question. Research.

He rode home with me even though this is not his bus and his neighborhood is on the other side of town. We didn't talk the whole ride, but then when he got off at my stop, I finally spoke up.

"What do you want from me? Why are you following me?"

"Can we talk?" he asked so quietly that I could hardly hear what he said. "Just five minutes?"

I sat down on the wall at the end of my driveway and he sat next to me. We ended up staying there hearing each other's stories for more than an hour, till my mom pulled into the driveway. She ended up driving him home.

I shared Manuel's whole story with my mom and dad during dinner. His life was so different than mine. So very different. His father died last year, after somebody stabbed him at work. His mom moved them here to get away from that environment, and she had been working two jobs till she got sick. His sister is a senior in high school and wants to go to college but life is tough right now. He showed me a picture on his phone of his mom, his dad, and his sister. I recognized her right away. She works after school at the mall. At LotusBlossom. The girl he was with the night I saw him and thought he had a girlfriend.

The more we talked, the more I understood. Manuel wanted a friend he could talk to and he thought from the very first day he saw me and called me New Girl that I could be that friend. He said there was something different about me. A kind heart. An open mind. A poet's perspective.

Then he handed the poem I had written back to me, and said, "I really tried but I just don't get it. What does this poem have to do with me?"

I read it out loud.

Be careful what you do in the dark
When you think no one is watching
Be careful you don't break a heart
When you're trying to play it so cool

"I made a big mistake," I said. "I think I actually wrote this poem for me. I'll write you a new one tomorrow."

That's when my mom pulled up and volunteered to drive him home. That's when my mom, Marsha Malcolm, Attorney at Law, began her quest to represent the Garcia family in their wrongful death lawsuit and put a criminal behind bars. And that's when Manuel Garcia and Elinor Malcolm, two poets and classmates, became actual friends.

FORTY-FOUR

Namaste

In the week leading up to the garden party, Martin had been busy planting white hydrangeas and calla lilies and sweet alyssum between the magnolia tree and the beautiful moonflower vine that Christine and I saw him delivering the day we discovered the suitcases missing from the shed. He hung strings of lights along the fence and across the garden trellis, and filled the birdbath and all the birdfeeders. Christine came over and helped me install the poetry walk along the path that Martin had decorated with tiny white pebbles.

We had built the poetry walk with the scrap wood Christine's dad had stored in his garage. He helped us sand and paint six wooden posts, one for each line of my poem. Then I painstakingly wrote out each line with a thin paintbrush and Christine added perfect swirls and flourishes and illustrations to enhance the words. Christine's dad made a heart shaped sign that said *Grandma Ruth's Memorial Garden*, that Martin hung from the garden gate while we kept my mom busy in the kitchen arranging the food on wooden trays.

Before the guests arrived, we made my mom close her eyes and my dad led her out the back door. She stood there in silence with her hand pressed to her heart when she saw what we had done. "Oh, she would be so pleased," my mom said, squeezing me in a bear hug. "So very pleased."

My dad hugged me next and whispered in my ear, "You did good, kid. Real good."

We stood there admiring the garden, the three of us locked in a family hug, and then the guests started arriving.

The party had grown from a little afternoon gathering to a full-fledged celebration. In addition to Christine and her mom and Indira and hers, there was Liza Wren and her boyfriend who's a videographer, the entire yearbook team including Ms. Loveless who was wearing shoes and makeup, and Manuel plus his mother and sister. Oh, and our neighbors Mrs. Feinstein from next door and the guy across the street who I found out today is named Mr. Peabody. My mother had always just called him Old Mr. Crabby Apple. "It's about time that I got invited," he told me when I rang his doorbell to tell him we were having a little gathering. "About damn time."

When the sun went down, Christine, Indira, and I stood in the center of the crowd. Liza grabbed her notebook, her boyfriend grabbed his camera, my dad turned on the music, and we did our performance for an audience for the first time. My mom held her phone steady so Joelle could watch from her front porch in Tulsa, right across from the house my mom grew up in. A little poetry, a little yoga, a little spoken word, a little drumming, a little magical flute, a little singing. We had it timed and choreographed down to the second and when we were finished, we asked everyone to form a single line and take a little poetry walk with us through the garden.

Martin had even installed a little solar light at the base of each poetry post, lighting up my words. As we walked along, we recited my poem together.

In the garden
We notice life
A tree, a blossom, a buzzing bee
We are all connected
to each other, across the days,
across the years, across forever

"Here! Here!" my mom shouted as we came to a stop at the last post.

"Namaste!" Indira replied, making a deep bow with her hands pressed together in front of her like a prayer.

"To Elinor," Manuel blurted out, "The girl who brought us all together. The poet of my heart!"

There was an awkward silence, and then Liza Wren's boyfriend whistled and everyone clapped and the party was over.

After everyone went home and we cleaned up, I went back out to the garden. I sat on the bench under the magnolia tree and thought over this extraordinary day and everything that led up to it.

Liza Wren had announced at the end of the night that *Prima Yogarinas Take L.A. By Storm: A Liza Wren Mystery in Verse* was edited and slated for a spring release. So was *Evolution: Ten Remarkable Stories of Growth and Resilience.* My mom now has an agent for her memoir, and is working on a huge settlement for the Garcias. My dad is looking for a new job where he doesn't have to travel so much. I have real friends and a happy family who gathered in our garden together to celebrate life. And, the boy I like is a poet.

The moon was just an autumn crescent but it still lit up the night. The flowers were glowing in our moon garden. The leaves on the trees were whispering a tree song and I could feel my Grandma Ruth's stubborn spirit there beside me. Everyone tells me that I'm the one who made all this happen. I brought everyone together. I'm not so sure though. I think there are other forces at work, pulling us together like the tides.

I stood up, following the scent of the moonflower vine releasing its nighttime perfume. "To the future," I said out loud as I bent down and picked one white blossom. "To the glorious, exciting, unpredictable future." I tucked it behind my ear, and breathed in the magical night while I stood beneath Grandma Ruth's Memorial Garden heart, dancing in the breeze.

"Thank you," I whispered. "For everything."

Namaste.

ABOUT THE
Author

Kate McCarroll Moore has been writing since she was a little girl. When she grew up, she became a teacher and a librarian and a poet and a mom. She never grows tired of people-watching and eavesdropping, using her writer's imagination to turn ordinary events into unique characters with interesting stories to tell.

When Kate's daughters were young, she spent countless hours dreaming up stories in the back of dance studios and recital halls while they practiced and performed. This story began, as many stories do, as an overheard conversation and a scribble across a convenient page. That's how Elinor Malcolm came to life. This is her story.

Kate grew up in upstate New York and now lives with her family in the San Francisco Bay Area.

Download an Educator Guide from
www.CityofLightPublishing.com

Become a citizen of the City of Light!
Follow @CityofLightPublishing